Christa's Obsession
F/F Sapphic Demon Romance
JP Sayle

Contents

Christa's Obsession

Can Wanda's trees and all those who dwell in the forest help a demon and a dryad find their way past fear and rejection to eternal bliss?

Dryad Wanda is minding her own business when she falls foul of a case of mistaken identity and ends up abused and traumatized. Her brother comes to her rescue. Only, he isn't alone, and the result of his actions turns Wanda into a blissful one—to a demon.

Except Wanda has no clue what has happened. Safe in her orchard with her trees, healing her outer body is easy. Dealing with the fear that dwells in her soul is not such a simple task. When Christa, a stunning female demon and one of

Wanda's rescuers, comes calling, the bond between them is instant and unbreakable, and one touch is all it takes to change everything.

The trees know in their roots that love dwells in Wanda's heart. But can she find the courage to accept that?

What started out as helping her brother on a rescue mission to save a dryad becomes something more eternal for Christa. The tiny tree fairy captures her heart in an instant. Christa is a demon who knows her own mind and goes after everything she wants.

And if that includes begging a demon king to help?

So be it.

Christa's Obsession is book three in the Obsession series and is a sapphic (FF), steamy romance, where even the trees have an opinion.

Reference List of the Main Characters

Dakata

Brother to Christa, you meet Dakata fully in Demon's Obsession (book one)

Silas

Dakata's Blissful One and Wanda's brother

Merihem

Dakata's best friend and Controller of the demon and human realm

Peni

Merihem's Blissful One and housekeeper for Dakata, you meet him in Controller's Obsession (book two)

Scott

Personal Secretary to Dakata

George

Cab driver for Silas's trips to the city and Scott's Blissful One, you meet him in the first two books, but his book is Secretary's Obsession (book four) coming 4th of March 2025

King Asmodeus

Demon king who is in the whole series and his book is last King's Obsession (book five) releasing 4th May 2025

Dougal

A powerful troll and Blissful One to the king and the longest forest dweller.

Benra – Luka

Siblings of Dakata and Christa (these pair aren't getting a book…)

Chapter One

Wanda

"You're going to the city again? Why?" The words ran through Wanda's mind, the worry for her brother, it breathed within her. And for good reason, it seemed. The conversations with Silas, her brother, gave her a strange sense of foreboding. Those senses never steered Wanda wrong. She always listened to them despite the fact she often couldn't explain them if asked. Not that Silas asked,

or would have listened to reason if she could tell him why she was concerned something bad was going to happen.

Silas believed in the good of people, and no one took her seriously.

She flounced off towards the river's edge, the evening breeze making her curls bounce around her cheeks.

Her green eyes glowed in the dying sun. It bathed her in an ethereal halo, surrounding her with its warmth. Her fingers ran over the blooms as she passed, offering what little she had left within her to the plants.

Dryads were supposedly solitary creatures, only bonding their spirit to a tree. Yet Wanda had never wanted to lose her connection with Silas. Their parents were long gone. Wanda alone had followed Silas to the forest where he had set down his roots, needing to keep her own rooted bond with him.

There she had come across an orchard. It sat on the far edges of the forest that Silas resided in, dying through neglect. The four peach trees, left to fend for themselves, called to Wanda's soul. Silas had already bonded with his oak, so his powers for healing could not be given to another tree, not in the way they needed to survive.

Wanda was unique because she had the ability to bond with all four trees without diminishing her gift. They would surely have perished if not for her willingness to share her magic.

By following Silas, she had expanded her family, something she secretly craved. Although she understood that no matter how hard she tried to cling to Silas, as with all dryads, he was destined for something else.

She loved Silas very much, but Wanda, the younger sibling, didn't crave anything beyond the forest. Maybe a burger or two, whereas Silas wanted to head into the city and sing for those who, to Wanda's mind, didn't appreciate the pureness of his heart. She witnessed the destruction and carelessness of those who came into the forest. They left behind their garbage and trampled over the plants with no thought to the life they were hurting.

Dougal, Silas, and Wanda helped maintain the balance of life in the forest and to Wanda, there was no greater gift. So no, Wanda didn't want to leave the forest, her orchard, despite what Silas said about those he sang for.

So here she was, fretting and terrified of all the changes that were happening in her small part of the world. Silas was a blissful one, the equivalent of a shifter's fated mate, to a demon, of all things. How this was possible, Wanda couldn't fathom.

Weren't demons evil creatures?

Destroyers of good?

Dougal, the troll of the forest, who was the font of all knowledge on such things as humans, shifters and all other beings, would have the answer, and all she had to do was ask. Only Wanda didn't know how to ask. To express her fear when Silas himself seemed—content—*excited* by this situation.

"You got somethin' on your mind, Wanda?" Dougal walked patiently at her side. As usual, he picked up her unease. The troll was perceptive.

She hesitated, then gave in, looking at Dougal as he walked quietly beside her like he had done a thousand times before. The troll wore a coat of many pockets. It never ceased to surprise her what he could find within it. "You're right, I do."

She sighed, knowing that talking to Silas about her worries wouldn't help when he saw things so differently to her. Her lips parted, then she stilled, listening out.

Head tilting, her curls tumbled around one shoulder at the voices that carried on the air. She didn't stop to think and took off, sensing where the interlopers were. "Someone's in my orchard."

The idiots were tramping around her trees.

"Slow down," Dougal called out after her.

"My trees need me," she called back, quickening her pace.

It wasn't the first time humans had come to take from the full branches of fruit. Wanda was happy to share, she just preferred they asked first. Her trees did not like anyone else touching them. They could get a little testy about such things.

"You there, what are you doing?" she called out when in sight of the two tall strangers, one of whom was running his fingers down the bark of the smallest peach tree in a way that left Wanda feeling violated. Her tree shook its branches, trying to slap the hand away.

Stop them.

Her trees' demand had her running when the big brute didn't seem to notice he was getting whipped by branches.

The need to get them away overrode all common sense. "Stop that right now. They don't like to be touched by strangers. I don't go poking around your home touching your things, do I?"

They turned as one. An enormous wall of muscled chests, or so it seemed when they blocked the light, towering over her.

Eyes as dark as coal matched sneers that made everything inside Wanda scream for her to run. Their presence was unholy, yet the need to protect her family kept her right where she was. Chin poking out, she did her best to hide her fear.

The sense she was in serious trouble came too late when they grabbed hold of her arms, jerking her clear off the ground like she weighed nothing at all. She juddered violently at the feeling of their hands touching her skin. The dread she had felt earlier deepened. It attached itself to her heart, squeezing it in a painful, vice-like grip.

Oh, to the forest goddesses!

She struggled to shake off the touch that sucked on the pureness of her soul.

"Great. The asshole got a dryad. That wasn't difficult." One of the men—demons grunted.

Wanda could sense the darkness surrounding his soul and her confusion at his words came with a slither of hope when she heard Dougal shout to let her go.

Violent shudders ran through Wanda, her stomach heaving and her eyes slamming shut as she felt herself leave the forest. The tight snap of the band severing her from her trees cleaved her heart in two. The pain left her gasping for air.

"Get off me, you idiots," she gasped, hoping someone might hear and come to her rescue. "Put me down, this instant." She kicked out her bare foot, and it was like kicking a tree. All it did was make her bare toes throb.

A hand smacked her cheek, the impact so brutal it made her head snap back. White spots danced in front of her wavering vision and blood trickled out of the corner of her mouth from where her teeth bit her lip. The throb of her toes didn't compete with the pain coming from her cheekbone, which she was positive that ham fisted ass had broken.

"Shut the fuck up," growled the one who hit her. They shook her violently, making her flap about like a shift on the breeze. A nauseating scent coming from them overshadowed the sweet smell of the peaches that lingered on her skin.

It was then that the air shimmered and more demons appeared. All of them naked, they came closer, sniffing and pawing at her. "Let's hope Rainer says we can play with her."

A demon licked down her cheek to where her lip was bleeding and groaned, sending terror through her soul.

Each breath dragged in the scent of blood, along with what she knew was death, degradation, and sulfur. The darkness surrounding her broke with the cast of red lights, basking the room in a creepy glow.

Wanda whimpered, trying her best to stifle the need to cry out. Here she would know no pity. Beyond the walls, in other rooms, inhuman sounds sent panic through her.

Flung down onto a chair that creaked and rocked at the force, the breath left Wanda's body. The room filled with yet more demons, larger, and scarier. Their cocks were hard, and they pushed closer to her face, arms, and chest. She shrank back, but to no avail.

Each touch painted her soul in misery. Wanda was flooded by a sense that her life would end in this room. She could only pray it was a quick death. A death that Silas would thankfully not feel, being in another realm.

"She's pretty enough, I suppose," a huge, naked, red demon said, coming closer with ropes in his hand. His cock was enormous and engorged, brushing against her skin. "I bet I could make you look better, though, riding my cock. That would give you some color in those pale cheeks of yours." The menace in his voice stopped her blood pumping around her body.

Wanda had no time to consider how to reply before a scream tore from her throat as a large fist plowed into her unmarked cheek. The bone beneath shattered. She lost her vision when the pain hit her brain, and she slumped off the wooden seat. She was quickly dragged back into it as the demons used the rope to tie her to the chair.

Demon laughter rolled over her, much the same as the icky feel of the place, plucking at her sensitive skin, looking for ways inside.

More came into the room, Wanda's vision flickering with lights as she tried not to let them feed off her pain and fear.

Tied to the chair, she much preferred the hitting rather than the turns they took, pawing at her, touching, taunting, and torturing her.

Endless pain sucked her to a husk. It came not only from their bodies, but from the separation from her trees. She had never left them since they had become a family. The broken connection left them exposed and her dying.

They would feel her pain, she could sense it.

She willed her death as her swollen eyelids drifted shut, and she sank into a pit of despair.

Chapter Two

Christa

The pull to Dakata's demon came unexpectedly, but Christa loved her brother enough not to fuss about the inopportune moment. Leaving the pretty brunette she'd been chatting up with a smile of apology and no explanation, Christa translocated to Dakata's home in the demon realm. She could easily sense a feeling of urgency like no other from her demon half. Dakata lived in the human realm. To be here, at this time, said nothing good would come of it.

As the air shimmied, Christa noted the arrival of her other brothers, Luka and Benra.

Dakata gave them all a grateful look, but Christa barely acknowledged that. She was far too distracted by the sight of Silas, Dakata's blissful one, who stood at his side looking... devastated. Pale, yet somehow determined. Christa was positive Dakata would not have willingly brought his blissful one to the demon realm.

Dakata was the first demon in eons to find a 'blissful one', the person fate believed was the other half of their soul. It was so rare, Christa and many other demons believed they were a myth. The demon realm, like the human would, would have its gossips, spreading word that Dakata was here with someone special, before he left again.

Christa had no time to ask questions when Merihem, 'controller' of the demon and earth realm—aka the bringer of death to those who crossed a line and hurt others—and Dakata's best friend, appeared.

"What happened?" he asked without preamble, his attention on Silas. Christa could see his eyes widen at the sight.

"Who did Kisha fucking tell about the blissful bond?" Dakata demanded, in such a way Christa's demon side got antsy.

What's with you?

Silence.

Was there something Christa was missing? Kisha, a demon who liked to gossipmonger, would never be one to cause trouble on purpose. He was harmless, as far as Christa could fathom.

"How would I know?" Merihem's expression grew dark. "Has he done something?"

"Who's this pretty?" Luka questioned, talking over Merihem, his gaze directly on Silas.

Christa almost laughed aloud at her brother's utter lack of tact and his apparent wish to get his face rearranged. He'd clearly not read the room.

"My blissful one, that's not why I summoned you," Dakata snapped, so hard his teeth clacked in the ensuing silence.

"Well, that's sad, he seems like he'd be fun to get to know," replied Benra, adding a purr to his voice.

Dakata seldom came to the demon realm, which meant that whatever the situation was, it was serious.

Realizing her brothers were trying to get a rise out of Dakata, Christa slapped Benra around the back of his enormous head, rolling her eyes at him. "Give over. A blissful one, if I got my demon school teaching right, is a sacred gift and I won't intervene if Daks decides to rip out your intestines and tie them in a bow for being a dick."

"You're all making a great fucking impression," Dakata snapped. "Shall we get to the damn reason I need your help? We don't have the time to sit around and fucking chat about Silas. Silas's sister, Wanda, was taken by two demons. Dougal said—"

"Dougal? Who's Dougal?" Luka asked, frowning at everyone.

"It doesn't matter who Dougal is," Dakata growled. "We need to find who took Wanda and fast because she'll not survive away from her tree."

Christa's demon side became antsy again.

What is with you?

Can't you sense it?

Sense what? Christa opened herself while listening to Silas.

"From the forest," Silas added quietly, as if that explained everything. Christa figured Silas was referring to being a dryad.

We must help.

What do you think we're doing here? Christa asked her demon side, not paying attention to the ongoing conversation.

Seeing Dakata raise his free hand and make a rude gesture behind Silas's back at Luka, Christa moved and gave him a slap the same as Benra got. Her demon strength was the same as her brothers, and she wasn't scared to wield it.

"I'm just worried about Wanda. Please?" Silas murmured softly, bringing everyone's attention to him.

"I'll do all the proper formal introductions later, for now. Christa, my sister," Dakata pointed at Luka, "Loud mouth Luka, and big gob Benra next to him."

"Hello," Silas murmured, looking at the last man in the room.

"And that's Merihem, my childhood friend," Dakata finished.

"Yo." Merihem jerked his chin. "So, shall we get back to the matter at hand if it's so urgent?"

"It is," Silas said, lifting the bow he held, as if to make his point. "We have to find her. She'll be so stressed it will use her energy up quickly."

We need to find her.

Christa thought her demon was on something, because its behavior was just plain bizarre.

"Do we know why they took her?" Merihem asked, looking at Dakata.

"They took her thinking she was my blissful one..." As Dakata spoke, his demon emerged and roared in fury.

Silas laid a hand on his arm. That was all it took for Dakata's demon to become calm.

"How lovely," Christa murmured, the bond between them evident in the way Silas stared at her brother. Christa had given no real thoughts to a lasting relationship with anyone. Yet...

Dakata glanced at Merihem. "Merihem, can you feel any new soul down here?"

Merihem's hands came together, palms flat against each other. His eyes shut and his lips moved as he used his demon half.

"What's he doing?" Silas whispered to Dakata.

"He's a 'controller' of souls in this realm and yours. He'll find her, I promise, and everything will be fine."

Merihem's eyes opened. They were black and sat in his deep-red skinned face. They were as scary as the black pit of hell, which Christa had once visited. "She's in the Dusken part of the realm."

"Fuck!" Luka moaned in complaint.

Berna shook his head. "That's not good, man."

"Shut up," Christa snapped, her demon emerging. She was as tall as her brothers, only more slender in the body, and her hair reached her ass, flowing over her breasts. "Can you pinpoint her?"

Her demon was ready to fight. Christa was still trying to fathom why, besides the obvious that her brother needed help. Not one to fight her demon side preferred to use seduction rather than her fists and claws.

"Yes. There are about twenty others with her." Merihem's eyes became unfathomable pools. "Guards, I suspect by the formation of them."

"Battle stance?" Dakata asked when Silas made a sound of distress.

"Yes." Merihem closed his eyes once more, and his hands parted. There, in the space between them, sat what he could see. It was an impressive skill available to the 'controller'.

This ability to project what he could see between the force of his hands was a talent only two other demons had in their realm.

Silas stepped closer, his hand reaching out. "No," Dakata murmured. "It's harmful to touch."

Luka and Berna came closer at the same time as Christa, looking at the image, assessing who had a death wish.

"Isn't that Rainar?" Christa spat, pointing at the vision of the biggest demon closest to... to the demon gods, was that Wanda? Fury darkened her eyes as her demon hands clawed, ready to rip apart anyone who had laid marks on the pale skin of...

Christa felt the shudder ripple through her, her heart pounding as her body heated.

No!

Yes, her demon purred.

"It appears so," Dakata answered, but Christa was struggling to understand what the hell was wrong with her.

Stop pretending.

"Silas, you stay here—"

"I don't think so." Silas gave Dakata a look that suggested he'd be spending precious hours wasting his time and energy if he argued. "She'll need me, so I'm coming." He looked so angelic, yet his steel will came through to all in the room.

Christa ignored the toing and froing between her brothers.

Who's pretending? Not me!

You know what she is to us.

No, I damn well don't!

Feel her.

Christa didn't know how to do anything but that as she stared at the beaten woman, who, despite the marks on her skin, was beautiful—captivating.

"We need to do a four point attack. I'll take out Rainar while Silas grabs his sister. Merihem, once Silas has Wanda, would you send them straight back to the forest? You know the location."

Christa's demon didn't care what the plan was, she just wanted to get to Wanda and Christa's human side couldn't disagree. She could wait to explore the reason why until she was alone, because she needed her wits about her for now. Dusken was the worst part of the realm. It was not a place where any decent demon went, and Christa had never been.

Following Dakata, they all translocated. There, in the shady darkness, the coppery stench of blood, lust, and death permeated the dank air.

Silas made a distressed sound as Christa tuned into Dakata's thoughts, a talent she had. She felt him search the darkness, then they followed him as he crept forward silently with Silas.

Within inches of the first guard, Dakata let go of Silas's hand and tucked it into his pants pocket to keep him close. The move gave Christa a moment of affection towards her older brother, who was being too cute for words.

The moment got lost when a millisecond later, Dakata broke the neck of the first guard, lowering him silently to the floor. He repeated the move three more times before they got close to the door of the rundown building. Its windows had been painted black in an attempt to hide the interior.

Christa wasn't into blood and scat play, but the smells suggested that was what went on inside. Christa held back the urge to rush in with an iron will—something she got from being the only girl amongst strong-willed brothers—at the anguished cries that came through the cracks in the wood.

Christa's lips parted in protest as Silas burst through the door, his bow and arrow aimed in the room. An arrow sailed through the air, but Christa didn't see if it met its mark as Dakata blocked her view. Then, Merihem charged in and went to town on the demons as all hell broke loose.

Silas leapt over furniture, arrows flying, heading for Wanda, who was slumped and tied to a chair in the center of the filthy room.

Christa had never been a rampaging demon, yet as she followed a blood soaked Merihem into the room to form a battle formation around the others, she was ready to rip apart some demons for daring to touch what was most precious to her.

The thought registered, but the direness of the situation as more demons poured into the room to protect Rainar held all her focus.

"Get them out of here," Dakata's demon hissed. The moment Silas and Wanda disappeared, he spun, his furious gaze locked on Rainar. "You are dead."

He would be, but only after he'd suffered for laying hands on Wanda. He would know pain, and she was just the demon to help deliver it!

Chapter Three

Wanda

Something in the surrounding air changed, she felt it despite how she struggled to surface from the darkness.

Silas.

She struggled to open her glassy eyes. To check this wasn't a cruel trick of fate. His arms were as familiar as her trees' branches, and she whimpered at the touch of them. She felt her bond to him give back some of what the demons had stolen.

Relief came with wave after wave of pain as the scent of the forest filled her nose when she took a ragged inhale into lungs that burned from the effort. She was unable to form words with how weak she was. The rocking of her body against Silas's felt surreal, yet the pain told her she was alive.

It wasn't until Silas got her to the edge of the forest, quite close to the road, that Wanda felt herself being welcomed by her trees. The living bond came through the roots and soil that Silas now ran across.

Their love, all four trees' bond with Wanda, allowed the air to sink deeper inside of her, to the part that had suffered the most from the break of their connection. The love and care she had given to them, they now returned.

Their devotion to her was in the sway of the branches as they reached for her. The lush green leaves roamed her battered body, removing her dress, seeking her wounds and tending to them.

Through their bond, Wanda felt the pain her peach trees had suffered, yet they used their magic to heal her. Their love was unconditional, as hers was to them. What she'd been through—the shock and pain she had experienced—they suffered, too. That was the nature of a dryad bond and though Wanda hated that they had endured her pain, she could not regret their bond when they offered everything they were to heal her.

They made room for Silas in the nest, knowing she needed him to help her heal, too. All the trees combined their branches to create a canopy and block out the outside world. They covered her in leaves, cocooning her. Despite that, Wanda felt their sorrow that they could do no more to take her fear.

This is what I need. Your loving embrace. The feel of your touch, my beloveds.

You are the heart of us, Wanda. They…

I know.

She sighed, the pain easing with each loving touch. The words were unnecessary when they all knew what would have happened if she had died. They would have, too.

Her brother ever so gently wrapped his arms around her and Wanda felt his healing power combine with that of her trees. The gift was a precious one when Silas had a tree of his own.

The presence and magical gift from her trees and Silas worked in unison to heal the damage. Silas wouldn't get the same energies from her trees as he did his own, yet that didn't stop him from offering his dryad magic. His ability would assist them and quicken the healing for them all.

She breathed in the natural scents in the air, listening to her trees whisper of their love for her. It soothed the ragged effects on her soul.

Time passed and Silas stayed, holding her as her trees did. They all fed her with the life force of nature, healing her bones, her skin, and lastly, the slice to her heart.

Silas lay silent, but Wanda, as she regained her life force, felt his unease. His worry.

Attuned to Silas, she understood where his thoughts lay. Wanda tapped the hand resting gently on her thigh.

"I don't hate him, you know," she said, her voice barely a whisper.

"Dakata? I only wish they had found me down by the river instead..."

She understood now that Dougal must have alerted Silas to what had happened.

"No." Her throat was dry from the screams she had no desire to remember. She closed her eyes, requesting a glass of peach juice from her trees. A tingle of magic came with a slim glass filling her hand.

Eyes opening, she offered thanks before taking a sip. The sweetness and love within the peaches eased the tightness inside her.

She gave Silas a sad smile. "You will not think like that. None of this was on you, or your demon, or the bond you've made with him. Your bond was clearly inevitable, natural, and meant to be. My being taken resulted from someone else's foolishness."

"I don't understand." Silas winced, and Wanda got a feeling of his inner conflict.

"I heard the ringleader talking." Wanda chuckled tiredly. Talking, no, it was more screaming while they...

She closed out the violent images. "Honestly, those thugs didn't have two brain cells to rub together..." She relayed what she had heard. Making sure to keep everything else inside her, because Silas wasn't guilty of anything. It was Fate herself that had marked him for his demon, despite the raving of those in the other realm.

"Do I want to know what Dakata has done?"

Silas didn't sound like he did, but Wanda knew he needed to hear what those big thugs had said. "Yes, you need to know..." Repeating it helped when Silas lost the creases of worry that marred his forehead.

She answered all his questions, even as they reminded her of what those monsters had planned for her. "The biggest crime, according to the ringleader, was that Dakata thought himself far superior to everyone else because he didn't spend his time in their realm engaging in endless orgies."

Those same orgies they planned for her. Something else Silas didn't need to know.

"Are you sure you're all right? They didn't do anything... you know. Your shift got torn, and there was blood..."

Her heart shuddered inside her. Broken bones, bruises, and touches that weren't welcome were her own burden to carry. "No, my dear brother. Remember, the idiots who took me thought I had a blissful bond with Dakata? Turns out that is what kept me safe. He wouldn't lower himself to engage in sloppy seconds, as he called it, and was going to wait and bait Dakata with the idea that he would, frequently, when your demon was dead."

The threats as they'd touched her had felt real. Only, the demons lacked the understanding that being away from her trees would not have given them long to do anything more. That was what Wanda had clung to at the time, as she'd waited for death to claim her.

"My demon needs to fight just a little bit harder." Silas winced again, clutching his belly, and Wanda realized that something was very wrong.

"You need to be back with your own oak," Wanda fretted. "I promise you, I'm all right, and if I need anything, I'm equally sure that Dougal is camped just outside my grove as we speak." She raised her voice, having sensed the troll's arrival minutes earlier when she got an additional boost of energy from him. "Aren't you, Dougal?"

"I'm not eavesdropping, if that's what you're thinking." Dougal's gruff tone let Wanda know how upset he was. "It's just, with what you've been through, young miss, I thought you'd like some toasted marshmallows, and a bit of lunch when you've had a rest. Silas needs to get back to his tree because his energies are all over the place again. It'll be because of that bond with that demon, I reckon."

"You need to go. I am fine. Promise." Wanda leaned up and kissed Silas's cheek, using the last of her energy to get him to stop fussing and focus on himself. Her brother was not selfish and put others before himself.

"I knew you'd come, and you didn't let me down. You and your demon both. Thank you." Had she known that? She couldn't say, but she was more grateful for it than she could ever express.

They'd both bear the scars on their souls for eternity, and there was little that could be done to change it. They both knew it, it was part of who they were.

"I'll pop back later," he said softly, stroking Wanda's hair before one of her peach trees showed him the way out of the nest they'd made.

Before his feet had touched the ground, the nest shuttered around her again, making it impossible for anyone to see her. Wanda felt Silas as he rested his hand on the nearest peach tree, mentally sending his thanks.

Wanda smelled the fire Dougal had set in his fire pit, far enough from the trees to keep them safe. She heard the whisper of words as her glass disappeared and she sank into the nest of leaves that rustled and murmured healing songs. Her trees called to the forces of nature to continue to heal, not her body, but her soul.

Fear slithered around her thoughts, but the softness surrounding her reminded her she was safe.

But for how long? Would they come back for her?

Chapter Four

Christa

"Christa, I said no. The notes that Dakata left clearly state the terms of the contract for Live & Die mean they have to play those ten dates. They can't now decide to do two fewer because one of the band has met someone and wants to stay in a city for a few extra days getting his cock sucked." Merihem muttered, like Christa was an errant child.

Merihem had gotten into trouble helping Dakata retrieve Wanda from Dusken. No one had the wherewithal to speak to the king and ask permission to run amok in the demon realm, killing multiple demons. For Merihem's part, he was now demoted to the human realm and if Christa heard right, had gotten assigned babysitting duties of her and Luka. They had both stepped up when Dakata needed to stay with Silas in the forest.

Things were changing, all because of 'blissful ones'!

Looking for a distraction, Christa rolled her eyes at him, doing her utmost to piss the other demon off. She did not need to be babysat by anyone and having a…

She turned to Scott, Dakata's personal secretary, who had come in to take notes of the meeting, giving him a smile that would further annoy Merihem. "He's got no heart."

"I've plenty of heart," Merihem growled, his eyes narrowing on her.

Merihem was a terror, yet his lips curved into a small smile that made Christa take notice. She could see, moments later, that he had zoned out on her. Working with him was turning into more of a nightmare than she expected. Something was amiss with his behavior. He had clothes on, something Merihem hated, and hadn't once bitched about it.

Very damn odd.

It's not him that's odd. It's you using Merihem to distract yourself from Wanda, and you know it.

I wish you'd keep quiet. Christa had become fed up listening to her demon half complain days ago.

She didn't need to ask Dakata how he had felt when he'd seen and then touched Silas to know what a damn shock it was to feel the very same urges.

What she was struggling with most was how to deal with it when those from her realm had done untold harm to Wanda. Would she accept a demon? Christa's demon half thought she would, but her human side wasn't so confident.

Directing her frustration at Merihem when he had clearly zoned out of the meeting, she snapped, "Are you even listening to me?" She eyed him, trying to figure out what gave him the funny expression he now wore. "You've a dopey look on your face. What's with you?"

She glanced at Scott, who remained poised, waiting for them to continue. Nothing about his expression gave away his thoughts. "There's something up with him, you see it?"

Scott remained silent.

Christa huffed, fluffing her hair. "Demons!"

"You do know you are one?" Merihem pointed out, not hiding his amusement.

The big demon gasped, and then translocated out of the office.

Christa glanced at Scott, wide eyed. "What the hell was that about?"

He shrugged, looking totally disinterested, his hand still poised ready to take notes. "Demons," she muttered once more, crossly. "Right, let's get back to the contract as it seems I'm making the decisions today."

When the meeting finished, Christa had a hairbrained idea to share what had happened to her with Scott. Then she eyed the uptight secretary. He was buttoned up too tightly for Christa to think he'd be a good sounding board, and discarded the idea. So she kept her thoughts to herself because she didn't know how to reveal that she had also fallen victim to Fate. Saying it aloud would make it all too real.

Alone, she continued on through the day, doing her best not to think about the desire to head to the forest and find out how Wanda was.

She needs us.

No, she doesn't.

They'd gone and peeked, more than once, but the trees still protected Wanda from sight. She was fairly sure the troll that sat guard had known she was there. He'd not looked towards where they'd kept concealed, but something told her nothing got past him.

Every time they had left, her demon's disgust grew stronger at her cowardice.

As they'd already had their rampage in Dusken once Silas had disappeared with Wanda in his arms, it was much easier to control her demon side—*possibly.*

We should have saved her, and you aren't controlling me. I have no wish to frighten our sweet dryad. She has suffered enough at the hands of rampaging demons to last her a lifetime.

We couldn't save her. We don't have the power to heal her! Christa snapped, hating the truth of it.

Christa had done her research on dryad's when Silas and her brother had found their blissful connection. Wanda was irrevocably bound to her trees. They were a part of her soul. Christa had witnessed firsthand the devastating effects of separation with her own brother. The blissful connection tied Dakata to Silas and the mighty oak in the forest. The three were one. They each needed the other to survive, which was why Dakata had moved to live in the forest.

He had resisted initially, even without knowing everything would change. Christa now understood his reluctance, and she had all the facts. To accept a blissful one who was a tree dryad meant tying oneself to a different life. Her demon side cared about none of it, and she nagged incessantly for Christa to return to Wanda and touch her to seal their bond.

I'm not nagging. I know what you feel. The desire for her, to connect with her and her trees. You wish to know what Dakata experiences with Silas and his tree, don't lie.

Honestly, some days you can be a worse pain in my ass than my brothers.

The tingling laughter grated, and Christa worked diligently to shut out the annoying sound.

Yet her mind returned to Wanda, and those who had dared to harm her. The only solace Christa had was that when she had smelled those who had laid their claws on Wanda, she had taken great pleasure in tearing their fingers from the knucklebones. Their screams gave her some satisfaction, it just didn't alter her situation.

The reality caused a clutch in her belly with the pure longing to see—*touch*—Wanda and assure herself she had healed and was safe.

Realizing her mind had wandered once more in a direction that made working impossible, Christa closed down her computer and tidied away the things on the desk, knowing that Scott would do it for her if she didn't. The demon was all kinds of fussy when it came to things being orderly.

Stalking to the door on six-inch heels, she collected her red woolen coat and slipped it on, flicking out her dark curls. Christa flipped off the light switch and exited the office, her luscious curves swaying as she tied the belt of the coat.

The corridors were empty, and the darkness outside the window revealed the lateness of the hour. At the curb minutes later, she considered her options. She had a home in the human realm and kept one in the demon realm, spending equal amounts of time in both.

The idea of going to the demon realm held no appeal when it meant she became cut off from Wanda. It was irrational when Wanda didn't know she existed.

Had she felt anything in their presence?

We won't know if you don't go and see her. Take something to show we're interested in getting to know her. A box of cakes, maybe? Chocolate?

I'm not taking dating advice from you.

She's our blissful one, who said anything about dating? Those other women you went on dates with... if dates are what you want to call them, they were only interested in—

Don't go there.

Why? They love what you can do with our tongue.

Christa's cheeks warmed like the sun had touched them and her body tingled at the thought of... *You're doing this on purpose. Making me think about touching Wanda's lush body.*

It's what is usually on your mind.

It is not.

With a thought, Christa translocated to the forest, her mind set on proving a point. She conjured a box of sweet pastries that she found particularly tasty, blocking her demon side. In her other hand she conjured a small bouquet of summer daisies.

"What would you be doing in the forest in those heels? You'll break an ankle," the troll murmured. He was sitting at the firepit close to the peach trees, which scented the air with their fragrance. Under it, though, was the scent of Wanda. A mix of peach and something soft and earthy.

"I came to see how Wanda is doing. I'm Dakata's sister, Christa. I helped to rescue her." Did that sound lame?

Dark, busy brows merged over stunning eyes that held Christa's gaze.

"Is that so?" He lifted a mug in offering. "Care for some of my brew? Wanda isn't up to taking visitors just yet. She may be in a little while, if you care to wait for her?"

It was a test. Christa couldn't say how she knew, just that something told her the troll wanted to see what she'd do. She stepped around larger twigs on the ground and perched next to Dougal on the log, who offered her a mug he conjured at her nod, of a sweet smelling brew. "Thank you." She glanced about for a place to put the pastries and flowers, then left them on her lap when the only option was the orchard floor, only then taking the drink Dougal held.

"I'm Dougal. Nice to meetcha, Christa." His gaze dropped to the box and flowers, his smile broad. "Something smells good inside the box. As does that pretty posy."

"I bought these… for Wanda," she shrugged nonchalantly and took a big gulp of the brew without thinking, due to feeling awkward—like she was meeting a parent of the girl she wanted to date—then coughed violently with an aggression that left her glad she was seated.

It's not dating.

Be quiet, Christa hissed back, while attempting to cough up a lung in the most unladylike way.

"Put hairs on your chest, my homebrew," Dougal chuckled playfully.

When Christa had herself back under control, she wiped at her wet eyes, careful to not to smudge her make-up before glancing in Dougal's direction. "I've never been partial to hairy chests, I prefer the softer curves of a woman."

There was a sound of a sharp inhale, and Christa's demon fought hard to escape when they looked towards the trees. There, in a hollow, sat Wanda. Cast in the firelight, her brown curls hung beyond her shoulders and held a crown of leaves. The long flowing, peach and cream gown had a lace trim that layered the top of the dress. The gown accentuated her small, pert breasts that rose and fell so fast her chest practically fluttered like a butterfly's wings.

Was she frightened of them?

Placing the mug down with shaking fingers, Christa clutched what she'd brought and rose to allay whatever fear Wanda might have. "I'm Christa, Dakata's sister. I came when… you know, to help," she finished, unsure what else to say, not wanting to make Wanda think of things that surely hurt her.

Beautiful eyes, the color of forest leaves, swept over Christa. "I'm sorry, I don't remember seeing you. Things were a little…" Soft curls swayed around her delicate shoulders as a branch moved and stroked down her arm. "Thank you," she finished in a soft murmur, staying where she was, more branches reaching to touch the healed, radiant skin.

"You're welcome." Realizing she was clutching the box and flowers, she took a step closer, compelled to be nearer and not only because her demon wanted it. There was something alluring—commanding—about Wanda's presence. "I brought you a gift… some flowers."

Wanda was beautiful before she smiled, but Christa lost all rational ability at the soft curve of lips into a surprised smile. "You did?"

Aware Dougal was watching, Christa resisted the urge to demand he leave them. Instead, she walked to the tree and offered the box and the posy of daisies. "Yes."

The brush of tiny fingers catching Christa's as Wanda took the gifts shook Christa to her very core. She never noticed the branch reach into her coat pocket, placing several leaves in there. All her senses honed on the dryad, whose eyes widened.

"What was that?" Wanda whispered, breathlessly.

"Our blissful bond," Christa murmured without thought or hesitation, because all her doubts disappeared in that one moment. Their connection snapped in the scented air, fizzling with life so boldly everything else became meaningless.

The fear that came from Wanda stole Christa's joy when it doused the air with its stench. Christa could taste its bitter flavor in her mouth as she inhaled.

"No. No. No. *I don't want it.*"

The words, said so full of terror, left Christa and her demon side crushed. Yet what Wanda needed most of all, was for Christa not to deny her.

"As you wish," she murmured past a ball of emotion. Working on pure instinct to protect Wanda, she ignored her own desires and how the action of leaving tugged at her soul painfully, she translocated.

In her home in the demon realm, Christa screamed until her throat was raw. Tears streamed down her pale cheeks. The merest of touches sealed her fate and she could not regret it, even when her soul became tortured with the belief their blissful one didn't want them.

They had been rejected.

She shuddered, collapsing to her knees and clutching the hand that smelled of Wanda to her chest, lost in misery. "What are we to do now?" she cried out in agony. "What?"

Chapter Five

Wanda

Wanda couldn't fight her fear as the woman—demon—claimed they were her 'blissful one'. On some level—on every level—she had sensed that something bound her to the beautiful demon who had sat next to Dougal. Her trees had encouraged her to emerge, revealing herself at the soft lyrical voice that had danced over the branches surrounding her.

How could this be?

Why would Fate choose a demon for her? Why?

A demon.

A demon.

Shudders ran through Wanda, only now, with Christa gone, she couldn't figure if it was from the fear or from...

No, I don't want this.

We do, her trees whispered, their branches softening the blow by cradling her, giving her their honesty.

They hurt us.

She did not. She went to protect you, protect us, before she knew of our bond. You feel it.

A gentle hand touched her arm, and she jerked, dropping the box she continued to hold, that smelled of Christa and the sweet pastries inside. The daisies lay bruised at the base of the tree.

"It's alright, lass," Dougal murmured softly.

"Is it, Dougal? I... she... oh dear." Wanda buried her face in her hands, crying, the tingling sensation from Christa's touch continuing to resonate through her. The shock of it remained. Her lower body had reacted in a way that felt... *shameful* when only her trees had ever given her that feeling. She had never envisioned herself with anyone but her trees. Their touch gave her all the comfort—pleasure—she needed.

"My trees," she sobbed, feeling she had somehow betrayed them, despite their declaration.

No, beloved. You have not betrayed us, but shared yet another gift with us.

They wrapped their branches around her, ran their leaves down her arms, working to calm her. Offering solace. They helped with the unexpected tug of desire she felt lingering at her core.

Yet underneath it, Wanda could feel their disappointment at her rejection. She couldn't see how they could accept Christa after... *Would you accept a demon?*

She is yours, therefore she is ours, too. You bonded with us, all of us. Offered your heart and soul to protect us. She offers you the same. Speak with Silas, his mighty oak. They know what a gift it is to share in this way.

"Your trees understand far more than you." Dougal's tone was gentle, but she felt the rebuke in there all the same.

Wanda wiped her eyes, feeling the dullness of a headache looming, and lifted her gaze. "Those demons, they...

touched me. Harmed my trees. Wouldn't Christa reject me knowing that?" she voiced her thoughts.

They had sullied her.

Dougal shook his shaggy head. "I know what they did to you, lass, but that demon who just came callin', she fought to protect you. I suspect she was prepared to fight for you before she understood what you were to her." He tapped her hand, repeating what her trees believed. "A blissful one is a gift from Fate." He looked so sad, but Wanda didn't understand why.

"When you denied it, Christa listened to what you wanted. You might want to think on that, lass, because it would have given her pain." He lifted the box and bent to retrieve the flowers. His touch caused the flower's delicate petals to heal. He placed the beautiful, scented posy on her lap. "Might as well eat what the lovely lady brought, otherwise it would be a waste now, wouldn't it?"

Wanda lay naked, hiding in her trees, her mind full of Christa. Now that Wanda was alone, without the stunning outer layer no longer present to dazzle her, she could acknowledge the deep, inner beauty the demon possessed.

She had observed Christa before she had given away her presence.

The soft curve of her cheek. How the fire had made her hair gleam like polished stone hit repeatedly by water. The swell of her breasts underneath the woolen coat. Her scent, fresh and sensual. Her eyes, when she had turned, held wonder and desire when they had caressed Wanda's body. She had felt it resonate deep within her, even before they had touched.

She gave a mournful sigh at how those things were all Wanda could think of.

Her trees were very tactile with her, they knew her moods. They recognized before she did what she needed, from the very beginning. Her majestic peach trees were female. Wanda understood when they bonded, they would become her lovers. She never questioned it. How could she when they fed her soul with their energy through their touch? Through their life force.

A branch stroked up her thigh, the leaves tickling her flesh and bringing a rosy glow and warmth at her core. The sensual, slow build of arousal was something they loved giving her. Untold pleasure.

For Wanda, once she'd found the orchard, her love came easy. It was deep and everlasting. Tree and dryad. But she was uniquely lucky to have received the gift of four trees. Their branches, now strong, intertwined and made a space for Wanda to live inside them. She had no need for the house that sat in the orchard. Everything she required was within the branches of her trees. With a thought, and the magic she held from their bond, it gave her everything she could ever want.

She believed Silas had something similar with his oak, despite living in a house by his tree. They had never talked about it, and now she didn't know how to broach the subject with so much going on inside her mind. Was it a betrayal to want something other than her trees to touch her?

Silas had Dakata and his oak, so she could rationalize her reaction to Christa's touch. It no longer felt… *wrong*.

So wasn't it wrong to want more than I have?

No. Leaves rustled overhead as others fluttered over the tips of her breasts.

Wanda moaned, her fingers reaching to hold a branch as others parted her thighs. *She will give herself to you, to us, without question, now we have touched her. Given her a part of us.*

The words didn't sink in past the need building inside Wanda. The juice of a peach ran over her mound, between the folds of her sex. She moaned aloud, letting her trees distract her. She trembled against the leaves beneath her when the flesh of a peach stroked at her core, causing a flood of arousal to soak the fruit. The soft fuzzy skin, wet against her, left her arching up. Her sex throbbing with the need for more. Her breasts ached as smooth branches circled around the budded nipples and gently plucked them. They grew firmer with each cry of pleasure she released in their loving embrace.

We'll give you whatever you wish for, but know that Christa will, too, they whispered together.

Wanda moaned anew at the thoughts of hands, Christa's hands, replacing the branches and leaves of her trees. The pressure around her nipples increased, and she arched into their hold, her own desire soaking the leaves beneath her. Everywhere else, peach fuzz rubbed against her skin, massaging it. The scent of her arousal thickened in the cocooned world her branches created to protect her.

More juice trickled over her mound, the feel of it touching her throbbing clit almost unbearable, except it wasn't enough. "Please," she begged.

Our love, they whispered as a tiny fuzzy peach rubbed repeatedly over her clit, vibrations coming from the branch as it moved to her entrance. It teased her folds, dipping just inside, rubbing, stretching, giving her a full feeling.

Her body tensed for long seconds at the gush of warmth that flooded through her, before she melted back into the bed of leaves.

The stroking never stopped while she lay there, feeling not quite as satisfied.

It's not wrong to want more.

Isn't it? Isn't it greedy when I have you four?

This is not about greed, beloved. Your soul needs her as much as you need us. You will feel so much more with her, you'll see.

Leaves ran over her body, and it tightened once more with the promise. If she could open her heart past the fear, the rewards would be beyond measure.

If she could only believe it.

Chapter Six

Christa

The scent of peaches tickled Christa's nose. She inhaled, fingers moving restlessly over the plush bed covers as vivid images filled her mind. She moaned at the heady scent of Wanda's arousal.

Her dryad lay naked on a bed of leaves. Small branches teased pert breasts with pink, budded nipples. Pale, voluptuous thighs were parted, held open by larger branches, some of which stroked her inner thighs, leading

Christa's gaze to the triangle of soft brown curls that covered her mound.

Christa's body tingled with desire, and a feeling of wetness stroking down her clit made her gasp. She kept her gaze on Wanda. Could not tear her eyes from the beautiful sight she made with her arousal glistening on the folds of her sex. A peach was plucked from a branch, held above her mound, and squeezed. The juice trickled down the folds of Wanda's sex, but Christa felt it happen to her, too. It mixed with her own arousal.

Thighs parting, Christa arched up into the delight of the wet caress. Breathing deep, she could scent the sweetness, her mouth watering for a taste. The desire was there to follow the path the juice took over Wanda's clit. Dip her tongue into the folds and taste, then return to suck the plump clit between her lips. Christa's grip tightened on the covers beneath her as the desire built in her core.

Her own thighs strained and shuddered with the need for more of those delicate touches against her skin. She unclenched her hand, moving to stroke at her core, feeling her own throbbing clit as she used her desire to tease herself as she dreamed—because it was a dream, it had to be—of what she would do as the trees watched them. Touched them. Bound them.

The thought sent her flying over the edge, her body shivering as her orgasm peeked and she woke with a start. She bolted upright, her hand still buried between her sticky thighs. Her skin damp from...

Air shuddered out of her lungs so fast she couldn't draw it back in. The scent of sex and sweet fruit was thick in the air. Trembling at the possibilities, she pinched her arm to check she was awake. In the darkness, she could see nothing, yet if she shut her eyes, there was Wanda being pleasured by her trees.

Watch us, a soft, female voice encouraged.

She could not deny the demand, unsure how it was possible... unless she was in some sort of between space. Dreaming... yet not.

It didn't feel like a dream with how her clit continued to tingle with aftershocks. She brought her hand from between her thighs and licked her own essence from her fingers. She tasted... peach. With a shaking hand, she reached for the lamp switch and flooded the room with light.

Uncovering her thighs, she shuddered. It's not a dream.

It's not a dream!

Her eyes closed, and there was Wanda once more, her rosy skin glowing in the confines of her tree. Her limbs trembled as her trees brought her to orgasm. As they had for Christa.

Holy fuck.

A shiver of pure desire ran through her. If not a dream, then what the heck was it?

Nothing felt right. The dreams were the only thing that felt real. The trees… they spoke to Christa. None of it made sense. None of it. Her body responded, even now, while she sat in a club.

It didn't matter where she slept in her home in the human realm, the dreams—sleeping reality—followed her. Christa had tried to act like everything was fine when she really wasn't. How could she be when her body begged for sleep so she could connect with Wanda and her trees?

Today, as a last resort, she had rung Luka, looking for a distraction from her body's torments and the nasty ache inside her chest. It had become so bad, she was prepared to demand Wanda see her. Talk to her.

"What's with you?" Luka asked from his position at the bar next to her. "You said you wanted to go out and have fun." He eyed her closely. "You look like you did when I stole your last cherry popsicle when you were eight."

They had come to Earth Space, the club that Christa had discovered Silas in and brought Dakata to. Somehow that one decision had ramifications for not only her brother, but her too.

"I'm not enjoying the band," she finally said, having no desire to open up to Luka.

Dakata was the only one who would understand her problem.

But would he, when Silas had accepted him?

Go, talk to him. Ask him how we can make Wanda see we aren't like the demons who took her. You know her trees accept us.

Of course we're not like those demons. They were male, for starters!

Christa had a sudden thought. Was that part of the issue? She wasn't male? Silas's tree had male energy, she was sure, not that she'd touched it. Would Wanda's trees be male or female? The voice she heard was female.

How do they feel when they touch you?

Christa actually felt her cheeks warm at the question and took a moment to consider her answer, despite the voice she'd heard. She didn't admit that she had to think about it, that she hadn't the wherewithal to focus on anything when the dreams happened. Wanda held most—all—of Christa's attention when she looked stunning finding her pleasure.

Female energy. Yes, definitely.

Luka glanced back at the now empty stage, his brows drawing together in thought. "In my opinion, they were good. Not worthy of a contract, but pleasant enough to listen to."

"Look at you being all music mogul." She flicked her bangs away from her eyes, smiling at Luka, doing her best to act like she usually would.

"Shut up. I just know what I like. Anyway, your pouting has nothing to do with the band. Have you gotten dumped by your latest fiery flame?"

She aimed a hard, narrow-eyed stare at Luka that could shrivel a man's balls to raisins. "First, I don't pout and second, I have never gotten dumped by anyone in my entire life."

Did being rejected by a blissful one count as getting dumped when they'd not gotten past a touch of fingers?

What about the trees?

Heat flooded a different part of her. *Stop reminding me!*

"Whatever you say, sweet cheeks,"—he came forward and tapped on her bottom lip—"but if this comes any further out, you'll trip over it when you stand on those spiky heels of yours."

Christa hated he was right and did the only thing a demon sister could do. She bit the offending finger, hard.

"Fuck!" Luka yanked his finger back, looking at the bleeding tip. "What you gotta do that for?" he whined, then sucked his finger into his mouth.

"'Cause no one loves a smart ass." She wriggled off the seat and rose, paying no attention to the looks she was getting from men and women alike. "And as you aren't entertaining me, I think it's time I went home."

He made a gasping noise. "What? You wanted me to entertain you. Who are you and what have you done with my sister?" he exclaimed dramatically.

She raised her middle finger and then sauntered off with a sexy sway to her hips, listening to Luka's laughter follow her. *Asshole.*

Outside, she stood at the curb and debated whether going home was for the best. Her demon had other ideas, and a second later she found herself outside Silas's front door.

You're such a pain, you know that?

That may be so, but we need answers and I'm fed up with waiting.

Chapter Seven

Christa

She hesitated before knocking on the door in front of her. It wasn't like she wouldn't be welcome. She would, although possibly just not this late. But she had no clue how to actually start the conversation she wanted to have with Dakata.

The sounds of mumbled curses and the thud of feet on wood came before the door swung open. Dakata wore a scowl as he tugged his shirt into place. "What are you doing here this late, Christa?" he demanded.

Unable to resist, she rose on her spiked heels and kissed his cheek. "It's good to see you too, darling." She effortlessly moved him to walk past into the cozy living room. The herbal scent was subtle and didn't disguise the woody smell of the tree sitting next to the house.

"What's good about it? I was busy..." Dakata looked over his shoulder at the soft pad of feet on wood.

Silas appeared, a long flowing robe tied at his waist, which didn't quite hide the fact he was naked beneath.

"Oops, my bad." She winked at Silas, who smiled serenely at her, his hair a tumbled mess around his flushed cheeks.

"Can I get you a cup of tea? Something else?" Silas questioned, walking to Dakata and stroking a hand down his arm.

"She's not staying," Dakata muttered crossly, even as his expression softened as he brought Silas closer and wrapped an arm around his waist. "She can come back at a more reasonable hour."

"Don't be rude, my love." Silas rested his head against Silas's chest, giving Christa a look she couldn't decipher. "Christa has much on her mind."

"She does?" Dakata said at the same time as Christa answered.

"I do?"

"Yes. Now would you like a glass of cider? It'll help you both relax, then you can talk to Dakata about what's on your mind."

His ability to simply roll over Dakata's grumpy mood left Christa grinning as she took a seat at the table as directed by Silas, where she proceeded to watch the pair together.

Never would she have thought that Dakata would act the way he was. He was not someone to trifle with. For decades, he had built an empire in the human realm. He was a force to be reckoned with in both his demon and human side. The destruction and devastation he had caused in the Dusken realm would be talked about for centuries to come. His connection with Silas had changed his life... for the better.

For the longest time, she had enjoyed her freedom to seek and taste the sweetest flowers, never wanting to keep one forever. Witnessing the couple in front of her, she yearned for what they had. She had touched her blissful one and the connection between her and Wanda was unbreakable. The feeling of separation was real, almost as if she was missing a limb, or her heart.

How could she get Wanda to ever accept her? Did she feel their separation as acutely as Christa?

Being taught about a blissful bond and knowing no one in the realm who had ever had one left many demons struggling to believe they truly existed, including Christa. Until Dakata had met Silas. Then, as if in a domino effect, she had met Wanda and then Dakata's best friend, Merihem, had met his blissful one, Peni.

Silas and Dakata didn't have an easy start to their relationship. Was it the same for Merihem and Peni? She suspected it was because of Merihem's behavior.

Who would be next?

What did it all mean?

She didn't know. What she did know was that what they sold as a blessing was actually the most painful experience of her life.

The glass Silas placed on the table brought her from her thoughts. "There is honey in the pot if you want to sweeten the cider." Silas pointed to the small, brown-lidded pot.

"Thank you," she murmured, reaching for the glass. The scent of apple and something else came from the glass.

"I'll leave you to talk."

Glass in hand, she considered asking him to stay, then discarded it, unsure if she wanted to talk about what happened in Dusken in front of Silas. Dakata had explained at the time about Silas's connection to Wanda and how it hurt his soul. She didn't want to inflict more pain.

"I won't be long," Dakata said pointedly, looking at Christa.

She refrained from laughing when Silas shook his head and said, "No need to rush."

Dakata's scowl was back as Silas left the room. "Be quick," he muttered.

"Wanda is my blissful one."

Liquid sloshed over the rim of the glass Dakata had reached to pick up as he stared at her wide eyed.

When he said nothing and continued to stare, she sighed. "She rejected me."

"Seriously!"

"As a heartbeat, on both counts." She sipped her cider, getting a solid punch to her system, and figured that Dougal had to have made it.

Dakata's glass landed on the table with a thud, more cider splattering the wood, though he didn't seem to notice. "When did you... when?" he finished softly.

"When Merihem pulled up the vision. My demon side was—"

"A pain in your ass? Difficult to control?" he replied, sounding a little amused.

"Yes." She ran a finger up the side of the glass, staring at the pale, straw-colored liquid. "I didn't know what to think... I took some time..."

"To think? To resist?"

She met his gaze. He knew her better than anyone. "Yes."

He matched Christa's pose. "When did you go to see her?"

"A few days ago..."

"And?" Dakata pushed, his gaze holding sympathy.

"My hand brushed hers. She felt our bond and when I told her what we were to each other..." A hot ball of tears gathered in her throat, stopping her from carrying on.

Dakata reached over and cupped his hand around hers and the mug. "What happened?"

The soft request had her dashing her free hand over her cheek to catch the tear working to ruin her make-up. "Those demons that took her, do you know what they did to her?" she asked, instead of answering him.

"Beat her and molested her." His reply was swift, like pulling off a band aid.

Christa's hands shook, the sips of cider attempted to force themselves up her throat. Dakata took the glass from her lifeless fingers.

No.

No.

Oh, to the demon gods, no!

Wanda's vehement refusal of her made sense. She had seen the marks on Wanda's flesh, but she had not considered they would molest her.

"I'm sorry." The depth of feeling in those two words left Christa in no doubt that Dakata meant them.

"I know, brother. It's not your fault." She took a second to regain her composure. "Tell me those you got to first suffered in the most painful ways imaginable?" The malice was all her demon because she could think of many ways to make someone suffer.

He nodded before she'd finished speaking. "They did and if I could make them suffer again, I would."

She worked to keep her composure. "What do I do now?"

The shudder was visible as he lost some of his color. "You need to be careful. Staying away from her, her trees… will kill you."

Chapter
Eight

Wanda

You're being very naughty.

Why do you say that? Wanda's trees whispered back, sounding amused.

You know what you're doing. I... Wanda couldn't say it. Didn't know how to express how she felt about the presence of Christa in her nightly trysts with her trees. They had always loved to touch her, and she had found deep, immeasurable pleasure in their affection. But what was happening now was so different. It felt more… *intense*.

I don't need you to give me the words. I know my own mind.

What you know is fear.

The whispered words were the truth, there was no denying it when she hardly ever left her trees. She needed to be close to them and she understood their additional need to touch her so intimately. Renewing their bond much more than they had in the beginning.

Except, the touching had turned to…

We connected to her, as did you. Her body pressed against our branches, our leaves, her essence combining with ours. You sealed the bond when you touched her. Together, the bond formed because her heart is pure. It's why she sees you… all of you.

She's a demon.

Yes, she is, and she holds a blissful connection to us. To you. She needs us.

Wanda's temples throbbed with how her trees pressed the truth upon her. She accepted the truth, she couldn't deny it. That, however, didn't release her from the fear of how the demons had come into the forest because of her brother's bond with a demon. They had been mistaken and took her. Hurt her.

Dakata had enemies, did it not stand to reason that his sister had the same enemies? She knew Christa worked for Dakata's business, the same one that the demon had ranted about. Wanda knew she would not survive another visit to the demon realm.

What would that do to her demon? Hurt Christa? Wanda would never want that to happen... *ever.*

She kept that thought to herself. *What if Christa wants us to go to the realm? Visit with her family?* Wanda knew in her heart she would do anything to please Christa if she let her fully into her heart, her world.

She's already a part of our world. She watches us. You know this. She yearns for you. Needs us to survive. Listen to us. If you have questions, ask her.

How do I do that?

The branches swayed and sounded like they were giggling at her. *She is with Silas. Go see her.*

Wanda's trees opened, and she smelled the fragrant night air, full of promise after the day of sunshine. Flowers and plants offered their abundance to the night, while stars scattered the night sky and surrounded the moon.

The beauty of the night enthralled as it always did, and Wanda sat to admire it.

Branches nudged her gently out of the trees, and when her bare feet touched the ground, she got another little nudge in the direction of Silas's tree.

Go, talk to her.

Wanda didn't see herself as brave or daring, and this situation appeared to call for her to be both. What did one say to a demon when their last encounter had her pushing her away?

What did one say after that?

She sighed and followed the path, minding the plants and stepping carefully around the stones.

She had no call, as yet, to talk to Dakata. Would he think it odd, her turning up at Silas's door late at night? Silas wouldn't, but Wanda knew the demon had made the forest his home.

Would the stunning creature who wore tall heels and silk be happy living within her trees? Wanda couldn't see how.

She let those things worry her instead of the gnawing fear that came unheralded as she got further away from her trees.

We are fine.

That may be so, but Wanda was not. She paused and pressed her head against an old tree, seeking comfort as her lungs burned from the lack of air.

She felt Dougal's presence before he spoke. "What's this, lass?"

Wanda reached out a hand, and Dougal took it. "I... Dougal," she cried. "I can't do it. My trees, they have accepted her. They have bonded and they are struggling with their need to connect to her in... other ways."

She didn't look at him, not with her skin flushing hot at being so frank, despite the darkness.

"They'll wait until you can. As will your demon."

Wanda glanced towards the large man standing motionless at her side. "How do you know?"

He chuckled. "I know a great many things, lass. You need to have faith in that bravery and daring that you think you don't have. You do, and when you are ready, you will allow them to reveal themselves."

Hope flared to life, much like the plants at the touch of a hand to encourage them to find the light. "Do you think so?"

"I do." He pressed a gentle hand on her shoulder. "Do you wish me to walk you to Silas's for a visit? I can stay outside and wait to walk you home."

She hesitated, a buzz of excitement running through her at the thought of seeing Christa. *I can do this.* "Would you mind?"

His shoulders moved under his large coat of many pockets. "Of course not."

They walked side by side, Dougal offering her a small flask that held his homemade cider. "A little courage."

Wanda took it and had more than a sip, feeling a warmth spread from her stomach to her limbs and finally her head. With it came a relaxed feeling that she had been lacking, except after she found release with her trees. She nodded her thanks to Dougal.

"Careful, lass." Dougal's chuckle was a rumble as he took the flask back when she went to take another sip.

Silas's door opened before Wanda could knock and there stood Christa.

Long, flowing black hair gleamed in the moonlight. Lush curves covered in silk that clung to firm breasts left Wanda's body reacting much as it did at the touch of her trees. Christa was so much taller than Wanda, she had to tilt her head back to look into her eyes. Emotions, too many to consider what they all meant, flitted over her beautiful face. But there were stains on her cheeks that looked like tears. The cider made Wanda loose-limbed and maybe just a little braver.

"Hello," she whispered shyly, dipping her gaze when her nipples budded at the slow, sultry smile that appeared on Christa's face. The fear, for now, didn't come. Wanda wondered if her body had other things to focus on, like Christa's alluring presence.

"Hello Wanda, this is a lovely surprise... did you come..." Christa sighed and said no more, making Wanda want to ask her to finish as she searched her gaze.

Behind Christa, Silas appeared, concern clear in his furrowed brow. "Wanda," Silas murmured, slipping past Christa to kiss her warm cheek. "Are you well?"

She got up onto her tiptoes to kiss Silas's cheek, feeling the weight of Christa's gaze. "I am. I thought I'd pay you a visit, as it is such a lovely night." She glanced at Dougal, who stood silently watching, and gave him a warm smile. "And I have such a wonderful escort to keep me safe."

She knew the moment the words left her lips they were a mistake, because she had allowed some of the fear to come through.

"It was wonderful to see you again, Wanda." Christa's smile held pain before she could remove it. "I've taken up enough of your time." Christa nodded at everyone and, a moment later, was gone. Only her scent lingered in the air.

Wanda's shoulders slumped. "Why did I have to say that?" she moaned.

"Do you want to tell me what you mean by that?" Silas asked, but Wanda knew her brother.

"You know."

He stroked a gentle hand down her arm and took her hand. "Come inside. It seems it's a night for visitors. I'll make you a pot of tea. Then you can tell me all about what's on your mind."

Chapter Nine

Wanda

It was easier to watch Silas move around his home in a flowing robe than think about Christa. The familiarity of it helped lessen the weight of anxiety that came with the presence of the large demon who had, moments ago, sat on the couch with a laptop on his thighs, looking resigned.

There were other distractions, too. The scent Christa wore lingered in the room, along with her own distinct fragrance. Nothing like Wanda's delicate, sweet smell, this held sensual undertones… *sexy*. It awakened desires that Wanda did her best to keep hidden in her dreams. Christa's scent perfectly matched the demon—woman who held an air of confidence that Wanda had no hope of ever carrying off.

She was simple. Liked the simple things in life. She didn't want or need much. The clothing Christa wore was clearly expensive, much like her brothers'. Wanda could only imagine that her home had all those modern amenities that her trees lacked.

How would Christa fit into Wanda's world? Because Wanda would never fit in Christa's and that, along with the fear of threat, ran through her mind. Her gaze moved back to Dakata, who appeared unaware of her. Nothing about his presence screamed that he fitted in. And yet, here he sat, looking right at home.

Content?

Could a demon be such a thing?

A branch snaked over the table and leaves brushed over Wanda's hand. She smiled softly at the gentle offering of comfort.

"My tree senses your distress," Silas murmured quietly, placing the sweet, scented tea in front of her. "I'll ask Dakata to leave us."

Her lips parted to deny she needed him to leave, even though it was a lie, but Silas shook his head. "He will play on his laptop, so don't fear we are disturbing him."

Wanda didn't look directly at the large demon as he rose silently and closed the laptop, putting it under his arm before coming and kissing Silas.

She didn't look away, needing to understand how they fit. How could Silas not fear those who hated the demon, and those who threatened him? Despite what had happened, there was nothing in their embrace that disputed their blissful bond.

All she sensed was... love, deep and abiding. There was no fear—none. Their connection hummed in the life of the mighty oak pressed against the house. The feelings coming from the oak were of acceptance and the honor of having found their third.

Oh mercy me, you bonded with her.

"Take your tea, I'll follow you shortly." Silas pressed a mug into Dakata's hand before allowing him to walk away.

When Dakata disappeared up the stairs, Silas retrieved his own mug and sat next to Wanda. He took a sip of his tea, eyeing her over the rim of the mug. "I sense your struggle, Wanda. Please let me help."

With Dakata out of the room, Wanda gave Silas a wan look, working to collect her thoughts. Insulting her brother's blissful one was not something she wanted to do, but he resembled those who took her. She had not asked about what had happened in the demon realm, now she considered she should.

If her trees' lack of response to what she'd just realized was anything to go by, answers were what she needed. Her trees were persistent and must have given Wanda leaves—somehow. Allowing her fear to rule her would harm Christa. Could asking questions and getting answers help?

"What happened…" She sipped the tea to take away the sudden dryness in her throat. "To the demons that… took me?"

Silas placed his mug down and reached for Wanda's free hand. "They won't hurt you again."

In the fierceness of his words was sadness, too. Wanda came to the realization of what Silas had done to protect her. "You…"

He nodded. "Dakata… he…" Silas held her gaze, and she released a trembly breath at what he couldn't say. Taking a life, it went against everything they believed in. "I did too, to protect you," he whispered painfully.

She flipped her hand over to clasp Silas's, sharing the burden of pain he held, even as the branch which had comforted her moved to touch their joined hands.

"I took life to protect yours because they left me no choice, a decision I would repeat for you." His gaze moved to where Dakata had disappeared. "For him."

A tear rolled down her cheek. "I'm sorry." Life was sacred to a dryad, so to offer such a thing that would hurt Silas's soul eternally was monumental.

The strength of the blissful bond was never more obvious to Wanda as she stared at her brother, her own emotions in turmoil.

He wiped the tear away from Wanda's cheek as another fell. "They wanted to hurt my blissful one, and they succeeded with their actions."

"They took me, not you," she pointed out, despite hating that it happened, she would never have wished for Silas to have taken her place. No, she would never wish for that.

"Yes, but think, we have the same connection to each other as our trees, do we not, my love?" She nodded. "Hurting me hurts Dakata, and he unleashed his pain on all of them without bias."

Wanda gasped as she considered the number of demons who had been in the room with her. "All of them?"

"He has never spoken of it, but through my bond with him, I felt his rage. His need to punish those for causing my pain. It took him to a dark place that ensured no survivors."

"He did this alone?" She gulped, eyes widening, working to comprehend how one demon could fight so many at once.

"Dakata's best friend Merihem, his brothers, and Christa. They all fought for you, for me."

"Christa?" A memory worked free of the conversation with Christa. She had said she was there.

What Dougal had said floated through her mind, it all piecing together. *I know what they did to you, lass, but that demon who just came callin', she fought to protect you. Fought for you before she understood what you were to her. A blissful one, it's a gift from Fate.*

Was it a gift if it came with a threat of violence? A threat of death? "The threat—"

"Dakata erased the threat." The softly spoken words had no less impact with the truth behind them.

"Is that possible? Those demons, they…" Wanda had no words to describe the vileness of them, of what they had done to her. Something she would have to bear in her soul for eternity. "They were intent on destroying Dakata because of his goodness."

Goodness. He is good. Christa… is good.

Those thoughts lingered as Silas sat back, a soft smile replacing his frown. "They tried and failed. But I sense these questions aren't about Dakata…" His brow arched and the knowing look made Wanda shift in her seat and return her attention to her cooling tea.

"Christa, she's…"

"Your blissful one," Silas finished, when Wanda couldn't.

Her curls tumbled around her shoulders as she nodded. "Seeing Christa, here, everything about the demon, that woman is there in her eyes. I can't deny it. The sense of longing. The wrench I felt when she left—will she feel it, too?"

"She will if you have touched each other. Dakata has explained this is how the blissful bond, for the demon, creates an unbreakable connection. She bonded to your trees, also. Dakata and my tree have come to an understanding so he can leave as I do."

They had touched and still Christa had honored Wanda's wishes and left her, despite the pain it would have caused. Her trees had touched Christa too, *given her leaves to protect her.*

A shudder ran through Wanda as she acknowledged how selfish her reaction had been, even when done under the duress of her own fear. There was no way to excuse her behavior.

"I believe she would never harm me," she admitted aloud for the first time. Christa's actions spoke to the truth. Something Wanda's trees understood and now, as she held Silas's stare, she did, too.

How could she tell Christa this when she had rejected her? She would have to figure that out alone, and soon, to ensure Christa didn't suffer further.

Her fear of the demon realm and those who inhabited it was something else entirely. That was a problem that would need to be considered once she spoke with Christa.

Silas wore a somber expression as he murmured, "Sometimes, to protect what we hold most precious, we must sacrifice a part of ourselves. Don't let you fear diminish you. It will if you let it and it will steal your happiness. Don't let it do that to you." He rose and kissed Wanda's cheek. "A blissful one is a blessing."

Wanda thought of those words now as she returned to her orchard, waving goodbye to Dougal before slipping inside the nook that was her home.

Outside her trees, she was demure. Inside, she was a sexual being with needs. Would Christa understand that about her connection with her beloved trees? That as a dryad, she could never be parted from them or not want their touch. Would Christa want the touch of her trees? Allow them to bond with her as they had done with Wanda?

She is ours already.

Her sex grew warm and pulsed with arousal at how beautiful Christa would look, bound in the branches as they pleasured her. As they touched her as intimately as they did Wanda.

Naked with a thought, she lay on the soft bed of leaves and witnessed the branches open above her head to allow the soft moonlight to bathe her body. She envisioned Christa above her, watching her fingers trace the curves of her breasts, the silky skin pebbling under her touch as her nipples budded with desire.

Would Christa understand, if she could see her now, what she was offering?

She will know us soon, our beloved, we promise.

Wanda added her own wish to that of the magic of her trees.

Please let her not see me as sullied.

Chapter Ten

Christa

"We need to speak to Vince and ask if we can have the venue for an additional night. Tickets sold out in three minutes and demand suggests it would be financially worthwhile." Christa said, going over the list she'd created to keep her thoughts firmly away from Wanda. From the failed visit to the forest, and from what Dakata had said. Then there was what had happened while she dreamed after the visit.

I have such a wonderful escort to keep me safe. Those words had been on repeat until the pattern had broken with sleep and erotic dreams of a woman, naked in the moonlight, pleasuring herself... *offering herself to us.*

Please, I'm in a business meeting. Heat unfurled in her core at how much she wanted to believe that was exactly what Wanda had done. It was all so damn confusing. Yet, common sense wanted to prevail when Christa could not discount Wanda's fear.

Her fear of us is real.

Not us, of the situation in the demon realm. Go to the king and ask him for protection for the forest. To stop demons from entering that haven't had an invitation.

Christa's thoughts were halted when her demon paused, and a dose of alarm followed. *What is it? Is it Wanda? Has something happened to her?*

Merihem has been in an accident. He is fine, but needs Scott to go and assist with the injured cab driver, George.

Her worries got pushed aside. "Scott, Merihem needs you to go to him now. He's at the scene of a traffic accident."

When Scott didn't so much as lift his gaze, Christa frowned. "Are you listening to me?" she questioned, one shapely brow arched to perfection while she swept her black flowing locks over one shoulder.

"Of course." Scott gave her a sheepish look, one she had never seen before.

"Are you going to go? It seems rather urgent," Christa said with a little more force, hoping to pull Scott from whatever was distracting him.

He stared at Christa, looking like he was searching for answers. A smile tugged at the corners of her lips when his Adam's apple bobbed repeatedly, and it appeared she'd caught him out. "Merihem reached out. He's been in an accident—"

"What!" Up off the seat, his concern for Merihem was evident in his agitation, something he wasn't prone to revealing—ever.

"He's fine, as is Peni. They need you to go to them because of the cab driver, George. He needs to go to the hospital," Christa explained as she wrote on a piece of paper. She pushed the paper with all the details on towards Scott, doing her best not to allow her thoughts to stray back to Wanda.

Christa continued on and then sat watching Scott, who stood, iPad in hand. "Aren't you going? He's unconscious and has no one to advocate for him." She pointed at his tablet. "What are you doing?"

"He may possibly have healed before I get there. But I'm looking at the hospitals in the area, assessing likely courses of action for the paramedics."

"Possibly, but our guys are worried about the bear, so just check on them and him. I'll sort through what's needed here, so don't worry." She clearly got his reluctance. No one was as organized as the demon in front of her. She didn't think anyone could possibly compete with Scott.

He nodded, spun around on his Italian loafers, and left the room. Christa returned her focus to the pile of work, once more using it as a distraction. Dakata giving her the job had helped her. However, his suggestion of, 'go talk to the trees, they will guide you and your demon side with Wanda', was confusing.

Cryptic. When Christa considered the feelings of dread his words caused... unless he was referring to... no, that couldn't be what he meant. Had he had sex with Silas's tree?

Shaking off the idea as absurd, she delved into the pile of work.

Christa was unsure how much time had passed when the door to the office burst open and Scott walked in without his perfunctory knock. Christa glanced up, a frown tugging at her sculpted brows at his slightly disheveled appearance. "When did you ever enter an office without knocking? And why aren't you at the hospital?"

He jabbed a finger at her. "I went to the hospital, and the bear is gone. I need to find him!"

Christa lounged back in her seat, sensing the panic rolling off Scott, but unsure what had caused it. "I feel I'm missing something here?"

"Does Dakata have the cab driver's contact information?" he asked, ignoring her stare.

"I have no idea." Her perfect bow lips pulled into a thoughtful pout. "You'll have to ask him yourself."

She tapped her painted nails on the arm of the chair, seeing this as a perfect excuse to do what she'd denied herself all day. She wanted to believe Wanda's actions the night before, in her dreams, were real. "In fact, why don't we both take a trip to the forest to talk to Dakata, *in person*?"

"What? Why do you need to come?" Scott questioned, looking confused.

She rose and smoothed down her dress over her curves as she came towards him. "I'm your boss—"

"No, Merihem is my boss, after Dakata. You are an employee, the same as me."

Scott had made this point before, but Christa liked to quibble over such things. Her laughter was bold as she slipped an arm through Scott's and turned him towards the door he'd come through. "You are too easy, you know that? That snooty tone gets me every time."

"I do not have a snooty tone," he argued, but went with her.

"You do, and you love to use it when you're annoyed. Like now." She guided him out of the building and into the back of a car without complaint, making Christa very suspicious of the reasons why.

Christa gave the driver the directions.

"I need my laptop!" Scott declared, hand going to the door handle.

Christa reached for his hand, removing it from the handle as the car pulled from the curb, not allowing him a chance to argue. "Do you sleep with the damn thing?"

Scott eyed Christa with a look that spoke volumes. He was clearly pissed off as he shook off her touch. "Of course not." He glanced away, looking very shifty.

"What's wrong with you?" Christa tapped on Scott's forearm, bringing his attention back to her.

"Nothing," he snapped back, then visibly took a breath, adding to Christa's belief that something had happened between Scott and the bear. Could it be... *another blissful connection?*

"Your demon side giving you a hard time?" she questioned after a minute of watching Scott.

He met her gaze. "Yes."

"I feel you." Christa looked out the car window. "They don't always see that life isn't just black and white, that decisions come in an entire spectrum of colors that can make it hard to find the right fit."

"Life can be more shades than we can fathom, yes."

She didn't turn to look at him as she nodded. "Absolutely true," she murmured quietly. "Then why can't others see that?"

Because you need to show with actions that Wanda has nothing to fear from us. Talk to her about what troubles her and go seek an audience with the king. I know she wants us. You can scent how much she wants us. Her trees are showing you this. She showed you this last night.

She had scented her... the trees...

The night before, the dreams were so vivid. When Wanda lay in the hollow of her trees, their branches touched Christa as intimately as Wanda. Her heart beat faster at what the trees encouraged her to do.

The car slowed as they entered a rutted road that led to the drop off place that Christa had come to twice before when visiting Dakata. The engine died, but Christa didn't move from her position as she considered how to make her next move.

She's scared, we can show her she has nothing to fear from us. You've never given up on anything in your life, so why would you not fight for the most important thing in it?

I want to, Christa argued back, paying no attention to Scott, who she could feel was staring at her. *Our blissful one is frightened.*

Yes, and as I said, a visit to the king will fix that.

"Are you okay?" Scott's question held all the elements of someone who was really uncomfortable asking something so personal. He kept his thoughts and feelings hidden behind a wall, always.

She didn't look at him as she reached for the door handle. "We'll see." With that, she took a steadying breath and got out of the car.

Christa gave herself a moment to get her bearings. She had no desire to use her demon powers and freak Wanda out by just appearing, if she was outside her trees.

Hearing the car door shut, she turned to see Scott's nose wrinkle. Much like she'd seen Dakata when he was on a rampage, Christa was stunned by Scott's behavior as his demon emerged. She couldn't look away at the sound of his suit ripping at the seams.

Then, a pale blue demon, shredded clothes flapping around his body, his cock slapping about wildly of his thighs, rampaged off through the forest calling, "George, my honey bear, call to me if you can. I'm coming and I'll rip apart those who took you from us. I swear."

For a moment, her own problems melted away as she grinned and watched Scott's pale blue ass disappear through the trees, trampling plants underfoot in his haste. "I never knew you had it in you, Scott."

Chapter Eleven

Wanda

Sitting in the sunlight, enjoying her fruit juice, Wanda did her best to set aside the concerns troubling her, hoping Christa might come to the forest. As the day dragged on, she could only surmise her wish had not been granted.

The glass sat against her lips as another thought popped into her head. *Had Christa decided she wasn't worth the trouble?*

You're being silly. A branch ran over her ankle and gave it a little tug.

Am I? I've waited all day and nothing has happened.

Did she sound as miffed at the thought as she felt? It was wrong, when she was the one who had turned Christa away. Did that help? Not really. Her body felt ripe. Needy.

It was unnerving when all she had to do was imagine the feeling of Christa's silky skin sliding against hers to make her blood pump fast through her veins. Make her clit throb.

She has a job, does she not? Human responsibilities, no?

I know. I can't think past…

Her heart slammed against her ribs at the echo of a demon shouting in the forest. His voice rebounded off branches as he called out. Fear ground her thoughts to a halt. Held her hostage as the glass slipped through her limp fingers. Peach juice soaked the front of her dress, but she didn't feel the wetness.

They've come for me.

Hair flying around her pale cheeks, she searched the trees beyond the orchard, terrified of what she might see but unable to stop herself.

He's not here to harm.

The words floated through her mind, but the panic blinded her to them. Moments later, she became cocooned within the branches of her girls. They shielded her to the outside world as they had always done.

Will they get in? Please tell me.

Shush, my love, he's not here to harm you.

She felt enormous feet hitting the ground. It vibrated up through the soil and through the roots of her trees. The distance meant nothing with how fast the memories of what happened to her resurfaced. Wanda's heart raced so hard she trembled violently, cowering back, working to make herself as small as possible.

We swear, he's not here to hurt anyone, her trees whispered again while branches stroked over her trembling limbs, working to distract her. *You are safe. We swear it.*

The power behind the words helped as the branches continued to act as a distraction, slipping under the sleeves of her shift dress to slide over the tender swell of her breasts.

Her breath caught at the tweaks to her nipples, making her gasp and warmth gather between her thighs.

That's it, our beloved, feel us.

Her arms relaxed at their encouragement, uncrossing to free her upper body.

Focus on us. On how your body feels when we touch you.

She could do nothing more when they knew exactly how much pressure to apply. A branch pushed up her dress to get to what it wanted. A soft leaf roamed over her swollen lips, the hood of her clit exposed as a tiny branch pierced a ripe peach, coating it with pulp and juice. It remained suspended between her thighs, the juice dripping between her folds.

Do you want to feel it touch you? Or is it just the feel of the juice trickling over your clit you want? Do you want us to tease you until you need more? Until you beg for Christa's mouth to touch you like we cannot?

The words had as much effect on her as the trees' touch. Already anticipating their touch, she lost focus on the muffled sounds beyond the branches. Her eyelids fluttered closed as her dress disappeared.

Soft air brushed her sensitive skin as leaves floated over her, barely touching her. They fluttered in small caresses, touching her breasts and teasing her nipples until they ached for more pressure. Her voluptuous thighs parted willingly as branches captured her hands. Her fingers curled around the smooth bark and clung on. Each touch made her think of nothing but the next one. Where would it be? If they would merely excite or give her what she craved.

"Touch me," she begged. "Make me forget. Make me believe it's Christa touching me." She finished on a moan, lost to the vividness of her imagination, smelling Christa's delicious fragrance. Could recall everything she had done to herself the night before with the hope that her trees had cast a spell to enable Christa to see and she had willingly looked.

"Did you see me, Christa?" she murmured aloud, lost to the pleasure.

A dream spell had never felt so real, and in that moment, she clung to it when soft hands touched her foot and Christa's voice murmured, "yes."

A hand... a real, warm hand... Wanda's eyes fluttered open, and she gasped at the sight before her. Her hands clung to the branches.

What did you do?

What you wanted.

How?

Does it matter? She came to us.

The trees had expanded her nook and Christa sat at her feet, dressed in her fancy clothes, her hair flowing over shoulders and down her back in a black silky waterfall of curls. Her make-up was perfect and her lips looked as ripe as Wanda's peaches. She should have looked out of place, yet inside Wanda's tree nook, she seemed… *at home.*

How could that be?

She belongs to us.

The seconds ticked by as Wanda lay there. Wanda had little to no understanding about guile. She would have laughed if anyone suggested the picture she made was to entice her lover. It wouldn't occur to her, so it didn't.

Her surprise held her where she was, unsure what she should do or say, now she was face to face with her wish. Christa stayed as she was, silent and watchful.

Her gaze skimmed down Wanda, naked and vulnerable with the scent of her arousal and the wetness coating her thighs. She had no place to hide what she had been doing and she couldn't decide what she should do.

You don't need to hide. Look at how she admires your beauty.

On display, Wanda had no choice but to wait to meet Christa's stare when it moved back up her body.

"So beautiful," Christa purred.

Desire scented the air, and it wasn't Wanda's alone. Wanda understood that, except she could see something more in Christa's eyes… yearning. Christa didn't hide the need reflected at Wanda. In that moment, she didn't feel vulnerable by her own nakedness; she felt empowered.

She released a tremulous breath. "You came," she murmured softly.

Christa's ocean blue eyes held her gaze. "I did. If you wish for me to leave, so…"

Was it wrong to ask her to stay when…

Talk to her. Explain how you feel.

"No… I want you to stay."

We do too.

"We," she corrected, "want you to stay." Wanda released the branch she held and stroked it before she moved to sit up. Naked as she was, the move brought her a little closer to Christa, and she felt the warmth of her presence in her cocoon. She inhaled the sensual scent of her perfume. Both acted on her already aroused body. Her nipples tightened, making it obvious the effect Christa had on her. Wanda conjured a dress and felt her tree's disappointment.

I can't sit here naked—

Why not? Christa thinks you're beautiful and you are.

Cheeks flaming with embarrassment, she noticed Christa's shoulders droop and heard the small sigh she released. *Was she disappointed I covered myself?*

Yes.

Shush, I didn't ask you.

You never asked Christa either.

"Would you like something to drink?" she asked politely, feeling more awkward than she did moments ago. What was wrong with her?

"Please."

Her trees produced a glass of peach juice and offered it to Christa, who smiled in acceptance. "Is this made from the fruit from your orchard?" she asked, her nose wrinkling delicately as she sniffed at the rim of the glass.

"It is."

Wanda's breath held as she watched Christa take a sip, then groan in delight. "I've never tasted anything as sweet or delicious as this." Her gaze held Wanda's over the rim of the glass.

"I'm lucky. My tree magic allows them to yield fruit all year round."

Christa's lips moved into a slow, sexy smile, the ripe lips drawing Wanda's gaze. "It also has many uses... the fruit, does it not?"

Wanda met Christa's amused gaze. Did she mean...

Oh my.

The leaves rustled, laughing, drawing Christa's gaze up. "Are your trees laughing?"

"They are."

Her sculpted brows arched. "Why?"

The delightful pink of her cheeks surely had deepened at Christa's intrigue. "Because they think they're funny."

Christa didn't push, and Wanda was grateful for that when she went back to feeling uncomfortable, unsure how to start a conversation that would most likely bring back the shame.

When the silence became full of tension, Christa twirled the near empty glass in her fingers. "I can sense your disquiet. Do you wish for me to go?"

Wanda sagged, hesitating and clearly giving Christa the wrong impression that she wanted her to leave. She moved as if to rise.

"No..." Wanda took a deep breath and centered herself as Christa came back down to sitting. "No, I don't want that at all."

"Do you want to talk about... us?"

The hesitancy she heard undid the knots in Wanda's belly. "I do... but first I feel I must talk a-about... about what happened to me. What they did to me." Her skin crawled from the flash of memory that snuck in without her permission.

You are safe, our beloved.

Christa reached out with her free hand and placed it on Wanda's knee, giving her a soft smile. "You don't have to, I know what they did to you."

Wanda jerked as if slapped, her eyes widening. "How?" she whispered.

"Dakata. When I went to visit him last night to talk about... us, he told me what the demons had confessed to in the hopes of surviving."

A hand gently stroking her leg left Wanda struggling to focus on what Christa was saying.

"Unless you *wish* to talk to me about what happened, then I'll willingly listen."

Wanda sensed the truth, knew she meant it. A glass appeared in her hand and she took a drink to wet her mouth. A deep breath didn't quell her nerves, but holding Christa's gentle gaze did.

"I feel ashamed, sullied somehow from their touch. I didn't want it. Their penis's rubbing over my flesh, leaving their…"

Christa's jaw tightened, but her touch remained gentle even when anger flashed to life in the depths of the gorgeous blue of her eyes. "How can I help? What do you need me to do? I'll do anything you ask. Do anything to protect you so you feel safe."

That it would be the first thing she would offer eased the dread that Christa would reject her, knowing what had happened.

She will never reject you.

Wanda believed that in her heart when the woman in front of her spoke only the truth. "I believed when I found my trees—because I am different from other dryads, who only bond fully with one tree—that they would be my entire world."

Taking another sip of juice, Christa offered her an encouraging smile.

"My girls, we connected immediately... *in all ways*." Would she understand?

The beautiful, sculpted brows rose, intrigue was what she sensed coming from Christa, nothing more. "They are your... lovers?"

She nodded, doing her best to keep from dipping her gaze. "I never believed I would have—*need* anything more than my girls."

Chapter Twelve

Christa

To conceal her worry about how filled with conviction Wanda's words were, Christa worked to contain her emotions.

Does that mean Wanda doesn't want me?

When Christa had stood in the forest listening to Scott rampage off, she had noticed a sensation creeping around the edges of her waking consciousness: Wanda's fear.

Wanda's emotional upheaval slapped her hard enough to make her skin feel the sting, so she had run. Her heels left behind, no thought to anything other than protecting her blissful one, Christa's demon half took control. Thankfully, it didn't emerge, conscious that doing so might add to Wanda's distress.

Whatever their intentions had been when she'd come to Wanda's orchard, it was to protect, not to seduce. There, at her trees, everything in sight was normal. No visible threat, no sense of danger. It was when Christa had taken a breath into her constricted lungs she hadn't smelled fear, only arousal. The difference left her rooted to the ground, confused as to the reason for the change when she was convinced fear was what she and her demon had sensed in the beginning.

When the trees' branches had parted, revealing the hidden nook where Christa had initially seen Wanda on her first visit, her breath had caught at what she witnessed.

Wanda lay, eyes closed, completely unaware of her presence. Christa could only assume the reason for this was what was happening to her. The trees enticed with their branches and their leaves, explaining the smell that filled Christa's nose with each ragged breath she took.

The scene before her was the most arousing she'd ever witnessed—been a part of. Just looking at the woman displayed—and she was displayed—on a bed of lush green, clutching at smooth branches, left Christa feeling intoxicated. Branches and leaves caressed Wanda intimately. Her sex, her breasts, the pale, luminous skin which glowed with flushed desire. Everything about the tree fairy left Christa breathless, but more than that, she left her enchanted. The desire was intense. She felt the wetness soak her panties. Despite that, Christa's strongest urge was the need to cherish. To protect.

When the branches reached for her, to lift her inside, she had no power to voice a complaint that Wanda might struggle with her presence. When the branches closed her inside, the conflict became real. Wanda's smell, how wanton she looked. The shy, terrified woman was now a sensual creature demanding attention.

The need to treasure the gift bestowed on Christa overrode her immediate desire to touch, to taste. So she'd kept a tight rein on both sides of herself, doing the sensible thing, not something she was used to.

Now she wondered if she had made a mistake and should have given in to Wanda's blind demand while she searched for the answers, holding Wanda's stare.

Christa didn't know how to interpret Wanda's expression and her demon's impatience pushed her to speak as the seconds slowly ticked by. "How do you feel now?"

Wanda's hair tumbled over her left shoulder as she gave Christa a look that left her with added heat unfurling inside her. "Would it matter what I want?"

"Yes, it matters to me, to my demon half." A flicker of some emotion appeared, then was gone at the mention of her demon side, but Christa wasn't fast enough to catch it.

"But we are connected... you touched me. I'm your blissful one, am I not?"

"You are. You feel it, don't you?" Christa asked gently, terrified of spooking Wanda.

"We all feel it. You belong to me and my trees. They will want... you, too. *All of you.*"

Christa had seen how the trees touched Wanda intimately. Had felt them touch her in her dreams, too. Would it feel the same here and now, with Wanda present?

It will. The female voice floating through her mind was that of Wanda's trees.

Is this what she really wants? Christa had to know when Wanda wasn't giving much away.

Do you understand we are all one? We will share with you, because she wants you to touch her as we do.

How?

We will show you if you accept us all.

Holding Wanda's stare, Christa didn't hesitate. "I accept you all."

Wanda released a put-upon sigh. "My trees, they are impatient."

Christa's laughter was bold and shook the surrounding leaves.

"You accept my trees too? Our bond? Their touch and mine... together?" Wanda's voice deepened, her eyes glowed, and in their depth, Christa saw the essence of her dryad spirit.

Her sex grew wet with arousal at what they meant.

Your scent entices us. All of us. We want to see your demon.

"My trees are very..."

"Chatty?" Christa supplied impishly when Wanda's blush deepened.

"Persistent is more apt."

"Do you wish to see my demon half?" Her demon side was all for it. Wanda's hesitation was brief but noticeable before she nodded. "Are you sure?"

"Yes... yes we are."

When Wanda included the trees, Christa's demon didn't wait for a second invitation. The tree branches altered to accommodate her size. They shifted without clothes, their hair flowing over her ample breasts, her hips nestled against the surprisingly lush leaves as she sat cross-legged, revealing all of herself to Wanda.

Did you have to sit like that?

It's comfortable, her demon replied.

You're flirting.

Maybe.

We like it, the trees murmured.

See.

"You're big…" Wanda said, not moving away now they were closer, knees nearly touching.

"In this form, yes. I'm the same size as my brothers. Is it off-putting?" *Please don't let it be.*

Christa's human side didn't share her thoughts, waiting and watching Wanda carefully for any fear so she could shift back if needed.

"No... no it's not." Her gaze moved up to where Christa's horns were. "Is there a reason for the silver tips on your horns?"

She leaned closer, flicking her hair over her shoulder when it fell forward. "They hold my strength."

Wanda's eyes were no longer on the horns, but on Christa's bare breasts.

"Do you want to touch?" Christa's demon was referring to the horns.

Wanda chewed on her bottom lip, lifting a hand, trailing a finger over the dark red nipple closest to her.

"N..." *Don't you say a word to put her off.*

Christa shivered at how the simple touch amplified the arousal humming through her from earlier. She couldn't swallow with how much she wanted those tiny hands to keep exploring.

Wanda made a noise in her throat, much like a moan. "Your skin is so silky soft. Your scent, it..." More blushing as her tiny fingertip ran over the tip of Christa's nipple, causing a fresh flood of desire and it to tighten. "Makes me want to..."

Christa waited, then, when she realized Wanda wasn't going to say more, shielding her expression, suggested,

"Come closer to see where the smell is strongest? It's what I want to do to you."

"You do?" Wanda squeaked, but the exploring fingers grew bolder, gliding over the warm flesh, cupping and taking the weight of Christa's breast in her palm. The abundance overflowed around small fingers. The contrast between their skin color added another element to Christa's desire. Wanda's pale skin contrasted beautifully against the dark red.

"I do. Can I touch you, too?" *Don't forget the trees.* "Touch your trees?"

"We'd like that."

The words had barely left Wanda's lips when leaves fluttered against Christa's sides, roaming down her legs, Wanda's gaze following the path they took. Wanda's other hand joined the first one and cupped her other breast.

She made these delightful noises that made Christa's sex throb. The desire pooled deep within and glistened on her inner thighs. Her body was hairless, so her desire was not concealed, if Wanda looked.

How Christa's human side felt about this differed from her demon, who wanted Wanda to know exactly what her touch was doing. *She might not like you being so daring!*

She does.

When thumbs circled her nipples, the bold move combined with the shy look she wore had Christa moaning, unable to deny the truth. Wanda wanted this.

Reaching for the hem of Wanda's dress, when she realized she'd gotten distracted, it disappeared before she could assist her in removing it. All the beautiful pale curves were back on show, and this time, Christa allowed herself to explore fully.

"You are so beautiful." Christa mimicked what Wanda was doing. Her breasts were smaller but no less full. The scent of peaches and arousal coming from her brought with it the desire to taste. "I want to taste you."

Wanda moved back, flushed with heavy-lidded eyes, her hands leaving Christa's breasts. She lay down, the bed of leaves expanding to make more room for them both. Christa became fascinated for a moment by how everything relocated without effort around them.

The questions she had could wait. Christa's attention returned to the tiny dryad. Tumbling curls glimmered as if threaded with spun gold against the green bed when her arms lifted over her head. Her eyelashes dipped as she parted her thighs, offering Christa a chance to gaze upon her in all her naked glory as she took hold of a branch. Her body displayed, each curve, dip, and line, was there for Christa to treasure.

"I could look at you always and never grow tired." Christa came forward and Wanda moaned at the soft skim of warm lips moving over her thigh.

She'd imagined this, but the reality was nothing as she imagined. The skin was as soft as that of a peach. The scent was subtle, not all peach. Underlying it, there was a delicate herb scent. Erotic and spicy when combined with her arousal that Christa could see glistening between her folds, on her thighs. "You smell so good."

Chapter Thirteen

Wanda

Wanda's eyes drifted closed because a part of her still believed this was an illusion. The gift she had thrown away in fear had somehow not vanished, and Christa had returned.

She lost herself to the feelings of desire for this demon. For the woman who accepted her and the connection she needed to survive in this world—her trees.

Warm, plump lips parted against her skin, and a tongue slid up towards the crease of her inner thigh. Shivers ran through her as the air touched the trail of wetness it left behind. Her body hummed in appreciation when Christa lapped at the essence which coated her thigh, inching closer to her center. Each lick sent tendrils of pleasure to her core, the wetness slipping free, making the leaves beneath her damp. She felt it. The heat of her own arousal throbbed in her untouched clit.

Wanda felt conflicted. She wanted to push up and encourage Christa to touch her more intimately. Having imagined her tongue on her clit, she wanted that, but also she didn't want the soft, loving caresses to end.

Delicate fingers skimmed up her inner thighs, then fluttered down to her knees and calves, stroking the soft skin. Christa moved back up the outside of her legs, repeating the process and making Wanda's skin buzz with flickers of desire as those fingers lingered close to her sex, not quite touching.

Her breath arrested in her lungs when thumb pads grazed the sides of her sex, deliberately pausing before sliding into her arousal and using the wetness to tease her clit, pushing back the hood to expose it to the air.

Wanda trembled at the delicate touch. At the feel of the air gently brushing her exposed clit.

"So good," she whimpered, resisting pushing up in case Christa stopped.

Desire was a bright light inside her, like the sun caressing her naked body, heating it degree by degree. Wanda's hands clutched blindly at branches, her moans escaping through parted lips. The branches wrapped around her wrists, knowing exactly what she desired. She wanted to feel their emotions, too. Her fingers curled into the branches, feeling alive. So very alive.

Can you feel how she touches me?

We do.

Her skin buzzed with the knowledge they were all connected. With each inhale, she smelled the richness of her desire as it slicked her sex. She could smell Christa's, also. It was stronger, but with more sensual undertones than her own.

Hot breath touched her throbbing clit, so close but not close enough, as a branch snaked around her waist and held her captive.

"Lick me," she moaned. "Please, I want to feel your mouth on me." Her breasts strained as other branches cupped her. They pushed her breasts up as if in offering. Then leaves danced over her nipples when a tongue flicked at her exposed clit.

"Oh my. Oh, my. Ohhhh myyyy," she gasped, held captive by her trees, unable to push up as the mouth danced away. Teasing her, teasing them.

The build of sexual tension growing inside her was like nothing she had ever experienced before. This was a passionate storm that thrashed and crashed inside her, leaving her desperate.

Mewling at the tongue dancing over the nub of sensitive flesh, her channel convulsed tightly, seeking more. So wet, her pussy made a squelching noise that grabbed Christa's attention.

"So wet for me." She blew over Wanda's sex. The heat with the wetness made her cling desperately to the branches, her lower body straining to get closer to Christa.

"What do you want? Tell me," Christa rasped sexily, more air hitting Wanda's clit.

"I need you," she answered, attempting to roll her hips up. "Want to feel your tongue inside me... your fingers." Trembles shook her as Christa delicately licked up between her soaking lips, stopping before she reached her clit.

The pause was deliberate, as if waiting for something. Wanda's eyelids fluttered open, she glanced down and became ensnared in the demon's gaze. Only then did Christa push her tongue inside.

Thick, mobile and so wet. The difference from the feel of a peach coated branch left Wanda's body clenching tightly. The groan Christa released vibrated through Wanda and overstimulated from these new sensations, she squirted over and into Christa's mouth. Her essence covered her cheeks, and Wanda's burned with shame. Her eyes closed to hide from what she had done, her body stilling. Yet, she couldn't escape or pretend how much Christa's touch affected her.

The hands touching her quivering thighs were gentle, almost as if attempting to soothe. But Christa's tongue pushed in deeper, lengthening as it thickened, causing Wanda to release a low, needy whimper at how it brushed over the sensitive flesh of her inner walls. Her body betrayed her as she reacted once more to the stimulation, her come filling Christa's willing mouth.

Look at her.

I can't.

You must.

Why?

Because she needs to know you want this. Want her as much as she wants you.

She did, more than she had thought possible. Wanda's gaze returned to Christa's. The air in her lungs got forced out in a shuddery exhale at the desire that burned in eyes that were almost black, the color consumed by dilated pupils.

She's not upset.

So silly, why would she be when you are sharing this side of yourself with her? Embrace it. Embrace her.

Branches released her hands, so Wanda reached to stroke her fingers down the demon horns to the silver tips. The tips, sharper than she expected, pierced the pads of her fingers.

The motes dancing in the air came into sharp focus as she arched into Christa's touch. Something fundamental inside her moved, like her insides were being rearranged somehow. She couldn't catch her breath and every nerve ending danced to a never ending song of pleasure.

Christa was unrelenting in her quest to wring every drop of pleasure from Wanda's body.

Moans against Wanda's clit increased as the tongue moved inside her, lips sealing over her sex. Sensation after sensation came with a force that left her trembling, desperate, and unsure if, when it stopped, she'd ever be the same again.

Christa slid her tongue free, using the tip to glide teasingly over Wanda's throbbing clit. It was divine, yet not enough. Despite that, she never wanted it to stop. Blindly, she continued to run her fingertips over the silver tips of Christa's horns, encouraging her demon.

Each noise that came from Christa added to the feelings building like a tidal wave ready to hit land. It grew deep in her belly, gathering like a storm preparing to unleash itself on the demon tormenting her.

Branches clacked together and leaves rustled as her trees shared her pleasure.

"I feel their need," Christa moaned against her clit.

A shuddery sigh escaped Wanda at the thumbs spreading open her sex, the tongue going deep again. It jabbed at her core, then alternated by sweeping up over her clit until Wanda's skin was dewy with sweat, her own essence soaking everything it touched.

"Ohhh," she cried out at the fingers slipping into her willing body. Different again from the tongue, Wanda felt her world turn upside down as her pussy clenched, wanting them deeper. Christa crooked them inside her, rubbing in a way that made the pleasure become more centered on her throbbing clit. Her palm rubbed her wetness over her clit as she thrust. The slick sound of her own desire added to the music of her trees and their moans of pleasure.

She couldn't catch her breath. Each fresh sensation flooded through her, leaving her floating in a web of desire that coated her skin with each feathery touch.

"You taste delicious." Christa's tongue lapped at the crease of her thigh and the maddening fingers continued moving in and out of her soaking pussy. "Everywhere I taste, all I get is your sweetness." Hot breath bathed her sex, the hand shifting to expose her clit. "I can't get enough of you, my blissful one."

Before Wanda could gain any semblance of thought about what Christa said, she cried out, body rippling against the soft bed of leaves, her core throbbing painfully as her orgasm burst through her.

The tongue pressed and rubbed sensually against her clit, prolonging the feelings. Color burst behind her eyelids at the purity of her release. It flowed through her in heady waves. Her clit beat in time with her heart while Christa kissed her sex, thighs and belly, calming her.

Heavy-limbed, Wanda's hands dropped and were cushioned by the leaves. Completely sated, her eyes struggled to remain open. Not an ounce of tension remained in her body.

"So gooodd," she slurred, struggling to stay present, then gave up as sleep claimed her while Christa continued to caress her gently.

Chapter Fourteen

Christa

Her awareness ebbed back into reality at the feel of a naked body pressed against hers. Blinking open her sleepy eyes, the dim light coming through the tiny gaps in the leaves and branches said she had slept some of the afternoon away.

In her long existence, Christa had never known both sides of her to be in complete harmony. If this was how Dakata felt, then Christa acknowledged that his actions in Dusken were more than justified. She'd understood it on some level, but now, after…

Her breathing became choppy at the desire to turn back time and make the fuckers who'd touched Wanda suffer again. That brief first touch they had shared gave them the blissful bond, but what they had done together—with the trees—had created a stronger connection that she felt in her soul.

Today, in that first touch, she'd felt Wanda's acceptance, and it took away the pain of the initial rejection. Alleviated the throb of despair in her soul. Wanda and her trees had shown her they wanted her in a way Christa had never envisioned would make her body throb with such an intimate intensity. If Dakata had suggested she would want the trees to touch her, she would have thought him mad.

She could not deny that each gentle stroke of leaves and branches had made her clit throb and her core become so drenched with arousal that the evidence coated her thighs. A sensory explosion while Wanda had been lost to her own pleasure. That the trees would bring her the same pleasure as Wanda made no sense, and yet it made complete sense.

We are her. She is us.

Yes. I understand now, Christa replied, feeling the branches embrace her and Wanda.

Christa recognized that it wasn't just her touch that aroused Wanda, that it never would be. Although they had tried to explain the familiarity between dryad and trees, it wasn't until she witnessed it that she understood the full depth of their relationship. The bond was deep, everlasting, and extremely sexual. Evidence of Wanda's desire for the trees' touch was there on her thighs, on the folds of her sex, glistening in the sunlight when Christa had entered the nook. It was erotically enticing to Christa, everything inside her coming fully alive for the first time. She had merely existed until that point. She was now an integral part of the trees and the fairy that lived within them.

What did this mean for her?

Can I leave the forest? Dakata had problems, will I now suffer the same?

The trees were as much a sentient being as her, as Wanda, so she aimed her questions at them, feeling like they would be the ones to hold the answers.

They rustled around her. *Silas has one tree, and though the mighty oak is one of the oldest in the forest, it is but one. We are four and Wanda is a special creature.*

That may be so, but it does not answer my question, Christa prompted gently.

Do you wish to leave?

She giggled at the evasive trees and how leaves stroked up her thigh teasingly. It was easy to recall exactly what they had done to her earlier. How they had restrained her and made her body heat with desire. The stimulation to her body left her moaning, and a part of her continued to be shocked by how easy it was for the trees to arouse her with such little effort. She had never had anything other than hands touch her before. Christa's curiosity, as Wanda lay sleeping next to her, became easily piqued.

When you touch me like this... she moaned, arching her spine at the leaves fluttering over her plump buttocks that gave her a reminder of earlier.

After Wanda's climax, Christa had sensed the moment she had drifted off to sleep, her need soaking the leaves beneath her. Wanda's touch to her horns, her blood coating the tips, made it impossible to ignore her own desire. She had lain down at Wanda's side, her hand slipping between her thighs, only to have it plucked away by a very insistent branch. The same ones touching her now.

Would the desire feel the same again?

Shall we find out? They laughed while warming Christa's skin with teasing strokes.

Wanda released a low moan, her body moving on the leaves, perhaps having felt something from her trees or Christa herself. She tilted her ass against the thigh Christa had between Wanda's splayed legs, her arousal slicking Christa's skin.

Breathing deep to calm herself didn't help when all Christa could smell was sex. Looking down at the arm she'd placed protectively over Wanda, Christa resisted brushing at the soft curls her fingers were within reaching distance of.

I fell asleep! Why did you let me?

You were exhausted after—

You don't need to remind me.

"You can remind me," Christa murmured against Wanda's ear, doing her best not to spook her.

"You can hear us?" Wanda squealed, twisting to look over her shoulder.

Christa nuzzled her cheek. *I can. I'm assuming it's because of your trees.*

"What did they do?"

We did what you begged for.

Their answer floated through Christa's mind, and she kept her breathing slow and steady to assist Wanda, knowing she was on the verge of a freak out. Her heart bounded through her body hard enough, Christa felt it beat against her breasts.

First, you distracted me, knowing Christa was in the forest. You got me naked and... A shiver ran through her as she broke eye contact with Christa. *Y'all are very sneaky. We're going to talk about this, but first you're going to explain what you did to Christa.*

What would be fun in that? We'll show you.

Show me?

Christa felt alarm, but there was desire with it.

"Yes, they can show you." Christa whispered huskily. The beat of her own heart matched that of Wanda's.

With the connection to Wanda's trees, Christa got the full sense of how Wanda felt about the trees touching her. The conflict came from missing out, not because she was jealous, and that made Christa's thighs want to clamp together at how her sex throbbed with a vigor that left her with a deep ache in her womb. Her essence slicked her folds at images that came from Wanda about exactly how Christa would look with her trees touching her.

Going with what Wanda envisioned, Christa moved back and lay on her back. The leaves were as comfortable as any bed she'd slept on. Those same leaves moved to stroke over her hips as they had done earlier. The teasing nature was as arousing as Wanda's attention as she moved to face Christa. She tucked a hand under her head, pillowing it, while her other hand slipped between her thighs in a move that left Christa conflicted because she wanted to be the one touching Wanda.

After we have finished, the trees whispered.

"Were you in demon or human form when they touched you?" Wanda asked in a breathless rush, clearly having heard what the trees had said.

"In my demon form, yes," Christa murmured through a throat that was tight from desire. "Do you want my demon to emerge?"

Yes. Her demon side was eager for it.

No. It's Wanda's choice, not yours.

Wanda gave her a look of approval from being given the choice. "As you are, please."

Her demon gave a dramatic huff, which Christa ignored when the branches took hold of her legs and spread them. Her bare mound hid nothing from Wanda's searching stare.

The hand between Wanda's thighs moved, her skin flushing pink.

"Let me see how you touch yourself." Christa's breath caught at the shy look Wanda aimed at her. She hesitated, remaining on her side, then shifted the top leg back, the knee of her other leg coming forward to touch Christa's thigh, giving Christa an unfettered view.

The sight of her pretty pussy, wet and glistening as a tiny finger ran over her clit in a slow motion, before dipping down to come back up wet to her clit, caused the growing desire to heat her sex to a level that left Christa on the edge of a climax.

"So wet... is that because of me?"

Wanda peeking at her with a shyness that was at odds with the picture she made while she bit her lower lip and nodded left Christa having to resist touching herself at the arousal flowing through her. "Let me taste you, please?"

Christa's lips parted as Wanda's eyelashes lowered, wearing a bashful look as she offered her a finger that moments ago had been inside Wanda. Without hesitation, Christa sucked it, licking off the sweet essence, groaning at the taste as she swallowed.

Wanda sighed as Christa released the finger now slick from her mouth. "Rub my wetness over your pussy and imagine it's my lips and tongue doing it. Unless…"

A look of expectation appearing along with a flush of pink rising over her breasts as Wanda shivered. "Unless?"

Christa gave her a sinful smile. "Come here and place your knees on either side of my head, facing down my body, so you can watch your trees touch me."

Wanda's hand jerked mid-air. The flush infused her whole body. "Ohhh."

Come on, beloved, she knows what you desire.

Christa found the trees' encouragement as arousing as watching Wanda hesitantly position herself over her face. The scent of her sex was heady, along with the sight of it wet with arousal, ripe and swollen, wanting Christa's touch.

The trees had other ideas. They captured Wanda's hands, the same as Christa's. *Watch,* they encouraged them both.

Branches covered in peach pulp moved into Christa's view. The juice dripped onto her face as they rubbed the fruit flesh over the whole of Wanda's sex. Moving between her ass cheeks to her clit, missing no part of her sex.

Christa opened her mouth, working to catch any of the drops as they fell from Wanda as the trees worked.

So caught up, she gasped in pleasure when tree branches squeezed plump, ripe peaches over her breasts, trickling the juice over them both. They rubbed pulp against her nipples, then down her belly to her mound. She arched in anticipation as she felt Wanda's heated gaze on her.

Unable to look down, she could only guess how she looked when branches moved and opened her sex. She groaned in approval at the stretch and feeling of stickiness that teased her lips.

She tastes divine. The trees' whispered words made Wanda's ass wiggle and her sex clasp, making peach pulp fall onto Christa's lips. She shuddered, her tongue chasing the peach, bringing it into her mouth. The combination of flavors left her straining for more. Her demon tongue, bigger, longer, reached where Christa's human side could not.

It ran over the branches, pulp, and pussy with abandon.

So naughty. The trees swayed in amusement, the noise much like laughter as they moved around them.

Not as naughty as you are for teasing us. Wanda's words came in whispered gasps as Christa didn't stop tasting, her own desire driven by Wanda's and her trees'.

"Ours," Wanda whimpered as leaves ran over Christa's bare mound, teasing the sticky clit as it throbbed.

"Is this what I missed?" Wanda's words floated around her, but Christa couldn't focus, couldn't stop what she was doing when her climax hit. It blindsided her with its force. It stole her conscious thoughts, leaving her no ability to do anything but feel. To immerse herself in how her body wanted everything, all at once, as she came apart.

You are missing nothing, beloved. See, our demon is beautiful when she flies apart at our touch.

In some part of her, she registered what they were saying, but Christa couldn't focus on anything other than Wanda's pleasure. Her body shook above her, her cries desperate as release coated Christa's tongue. The intrinsic connection made them soar together until nothing else existed beyond them and the trees.

This is all you will ever want.

In that moment, Christa believed them.

Chapter Fifteen

Wanda

In the cocoon of her trees, Wanda could easily forget there was an outside world, and it could be days before she felt the need to seek the company of others. Unlike her brother, who had a desire to see what was beyond the forest, Wanda never had. Dougal had kept away because he would have been more than aware of what was happening inside her trees.

In fact, she suspected the entire forest was aware of what she had been up to with Christa. They had to have heard her. She could not prevent the sounds of delight pouring from her lips. She had tried, when she had the wherewithal. For days, they had kept to themselves, discovering each other in ways that made Wanda blush and want to hide her face. She had easily accepted being the way she was with her trees, but how she was with Christa was something else entirely. A warm touch… yes, that made all the difference to the experience.

Wanda admitted to herself that she was still coming to terms with how her body hummed with arousal just being anywhere near Christa. She didn't have to touch her to make her want Christa's touch. To want the demon to appear and worship her as she had done just hours before.

Christa appeared to feel the same attraction. Need. And although Wanda was naïve, she was aware that only one of them lacked experience. What she had with her trees wasn't the same.

As if Christa sensed her inner turmoil, a hand stroked over her breast, and the tension bled away. She released a moan of delight at the tug low in her womb. As they were now, lying on the bed of leaves, looking up at the sky where the trees had separated to allow the morning sun to warm their bodies, Wanda considered life was pretty perfect.

Did Christa feel the same? Did she want more than this? More than what they had here, in the forest?

Wanda had no need for the things humans insisted they needed. When the urgency to immerse herself in Wanda no longer held Christa in its powerful hold, would that change things?

Since Christa had touched her intimately, the feeling that she wouldn't survive another moment without her lovers hadn't eased for Wanda. If anything, it had grown stronger. The hand on her breast squeezed gently. Her own hand remained on Christa's bare thigh, close enough for her fingers to graze her sex when the desire to reclaim the connection came. She held back a sigh at her own needy behavior, and to show her regret at refusing to accept their bond from the very beginning. To make up for those lost days, when she had denied them both.

"Your thoughts are loud, my love. There is no need to fret. We are here now, together," Christa murmured against her hair before untangling herself to ease up and sit cross-legged, a seemingly favored position when she wasn't lying down. Her hair was a tangle of black, hanging over golden skin that glowed in the sunlight.

"I'm sorry," Wander replied, working to keep the quiver from her voice and moving to sit in the same pose, facing Christa. The space adapted to accommodate the position change without thought. "I hurt you. I feel the scar inside you."

Christa's eyes clouded for a moment before she reached for Wanda's hand and placed it between her bare breasts. "Each touch, each caress, erases the past. Scars remain as reminders of how far we have come."

Wanda felt the steady beat of Christa's heart, hearing the sincerity. "Does that excuse what I did?"

"Fear is a powerful emotion. One I understand. There is no blame that lies at your door. It is with those who choose to hurt something precious. To damage—destroy a special bond. I'm sorry that I never met you before they…"

"Please don't," Wanda begged at the sudden wave of distress Christa suffered. "I would have been in the forest when they came, nothing can change that. I'm here, now… safe."

"You don't feel safe." Christa held her gaze as she let Wanda's hand go. She could do nothing but let it sit in her lap when she saw Christa's disappointment at the lie Wanda had attempted to offer. "I felt your fear the day I arrived. It was because of Scott shouting, wasn't it?"

"Scott?"

"The demon who I came into the forest with. He is Dakata's personal secretary, and it seemed he was looking for someone in the forest and lost control. He would never harm you. He's a real softie at heart." She held Wanda's stare. "All demons frighten you."

Wanda's curls bounced over her shoulders as she shook her head. "No. I don't feel safe like I did..." She needed to touch Christa, so she reached for her hands, so much bigger than her own. "But I feel safe with you and you are a demon. That counts, surely?" she begged.

The pause was so long, Wanda's stomach lurched unpleasantly.

"It does... yes." Christa's fingers threaded with Wanda's. "It's not enough, though."

A sob rose at how sad Christa sounded. "I don't know how to change it."

"I need to go to the demon realm—"

Panic, greedy and merciless, clutched her heart and squeezed it. "No, I can't go to the demon realm, I can't," she sobbed, upsetting her trees.

Christa let go of her hands and a second later, Wanda was sitting on Christa's lap, facing her. She cupped Wanda's cheeks and kissed her softly. "I would never ask you to go to the demon realm. I swear it," she murmured between soft kisses, which helped to allay the fear as much as the words.

Gazes locked, Wanda didn't conceal her fear. "I can't go back."

Christa nodded. "I know." She pulled Wanda closer until she could rest her head on Christa's chest, hand and leaves stroking her back. "I need to go there, to speak to the king."

Wanda shuddered. "Why... why do you need to speak to the king?"

"He is the most powerful demon. He can protect the forest from unwelcome visitors. Stop anyone not invited from getting beyond the forest boundary."

Wanda pulled back, searching for the truth. "He can do that?"

"He can."

"Will he want to do that... for me?"

A wrinkle appeared between Christa's sculpted brows. "I don't know."

There was no false hope, and Wanda was grateful for it. "But you'll ask him... for me?"

Christa stroked her hand down Wanda's face, brushing back her messy curls. "I would do anything for you." She kissed her. The passion that was never far away simmered with renewed life. "*Anything at all.*"

Christa's stomach grumbled in such a way it broke a little of the tension between them. She gave Wanda a sheepish look.

"Peaches aren't quite enough to fill a demon." Her smile turned wicked and heated Wanda's core. "Even coated in your sweetness."

Blushing up to her roots, Wanda had nowhere to hide with how close they were. Christa would not miss the wetness of Wanda's sex when it was so close to her belly.

Seeking a distraction, Wanda considered what else she could feed Christa besides...

They had no food delivery service to the forest, no Deliveroo or whatever they were called, that brought food to people's homes.

Christa's head tilted as she observed Wanda, hair flowing over her bare shoulders. She was beautiful in both forms. Her demon had more curves. Wanda suspected those who didn't look beyond those soft curves would miss the warrior beneath. She was there in the blue eyes that appeared to miss nothing as they swept over Wanda now, waiting for her to answer.

"Food…"

Christa ramped up the gorgeous smile and made all sensible thoughts flee. "Yes?"

"Food…" Wanda shook herself and shut her eyes to see if that helped. "You're hungry," she continued, making herself appear even more ditsy than usual.

"I am," Christa whispered, far closer than she had been a moment earlier. Wanda could inhale the sweet scent of her breath.

Her eyes flicked open, and Christa's face was inches from hers. "W-what do you like to eat?"

Wanda's pale skin burned with heat at the desire that darkened Christa's gaze as it swept down her naked body, arousing with its passionate caress and taking them right back to the conversation Wanda was trying to stop thinking about.

"*Food*," she stressed, embarrassed, yet pleased at the same time.

"What do you normally eat?" Christa asked, wearing a look of amusement.

"Mainly fruit and vegetables." An arched brow got her rushing on. "They are good for you."

"I'm sure they are." Christa's voice held a wealth of fun as she winked saucily at Wanda. "But I could do with something more filling right now."

"Like what?" The dip in Wanda's belly wasn't pleasant when she had nothing else to offer.

The question had hardly left her lips when there sat a large box just out of reach. The scent of mouth-watering melted cheese, herbs, and tomato made her groan. "Pizza! How?" she asked stupidly, because clearly someone had stolen her brain power.

Christa shrugged, moving Wanda so she could rest back against Christa's chest and sit between her now extended legs. She flipped open the lid and Wanda groaned in appreciation at the steam rising from the box, gifting her with more of the delicious smell.

Christa picked up a slice of pizza, folding the tip so the cheese didn't dangle down, and offered it to Wanda. "I can use human tools the same as everyone else, but I suspect a delivery service here is out of the question." She picked up another slice and moaned. "A woman cannot live without pizza, I assure you."

Wanda bit into the hot slice of pizza, the herbs zinging in her mouth as she moved the hot food around to avoid burning the roof of her mouth with the cheese and couldn't disagree, not in the slightest. She moaned in delight at the burst of flavors.

She grinned cheekily, twisting to look at Christa. "I think you might be right. I also like cheeseburgers, just so you know."

Laughter bounced off the leaves, giving Wanda a secret thrill as Christa let out the joyous sound. "I'll remember that."

Chapter Sixteen

Christa

Christa exited the tree dressed in a loose fitting shift so as not to scare any of the natives who might decide to walk through the orchard. What surprised her was the amount of humans that wandered through Wanda's orchard. The first couple Christa had encountered had gotten decidedly more than they were expecting when Christa had shifted and run them off. Wanda, who had been napping at the time, had woken with a frightened start at their shouting.

Christa had taught them a lesson they'd hopefully never forget. Never upset a demon's blissful one.

She chuckled at the memory of how the man had nearly broken his neck to escape her. Hopefully, he would tell his friends to stay away.

Checking once more that Wanda remained asleep, she whispered to the trees, *protect her, I won't be long.*

As always, beloved.

She took a moment to show her respect and appreciation, stroking her fingers down the bark, feeling their affection for her before she walked off towards the unused house. She needed a moment of privacy to make a call to Merihem. The conversation around fear, and her decision to go to the king, in principle, was easy. Getting to see the king alone, that would be more tricky.

Seeing no one was close by, she pulled a phone from her dress pocket and dialed Merihem.

"Where have you been?" Merihem demanded before she could even say hello. "Luka said you haven't been in the office, that you disappeared without a damn word."

A worm of guilt slithered in, and she held back a sigh at having done exactly that and showing a level of unprofessionalism that made her defensive. "You are not the boss of me!"

"I think you'll find I am," he fired back, sounding way too smug for Christa.

"I quit, I don't need the damn job." His indrawn breath was enough to put her back in a good mood, especially with the knowledge Luka was more than capable of doing her job and his own.

She had no intention of leaving Wanda. The very idea of doing such a thing on a regular basis did not sit well with Christa, for many reasons. The main one, even now as she wandered down towards the house, somehow it felt too far away from Wanda. She needed only to look back to see the trees in the orchard, yet it did little to ease the tightness in her chest at the separation.

As yet, she hadn't spoken to Dakata about this, but she would when Wanda was ready to move beyond her trees with Christa.

"—you can't do that."

The snap to Merihem's voice brought her back to the conversation as she worked to figure out what she had missed. He clearly thought she couldn't make her own decisions. "I can do whatever I like. Anyway, that isn't what

I'm ringing for. I need you to get me an appointment to see the king."

"What? The king? Why?"

"I need to ask him for something."

Merihem groaned. "I've just got back into the position of Controller. You know how pissed off he is with Dakata for his rampage through Dusken? Do you think he's going to want to meet with his sister?"

"Probably not, and yes, I heard you got your job back." Being able to read Dakata's thoughts came in handy from time to time. "I'm pleased for you. I still need you to go ask him to see me," she wheedled. "It's vitally important."

It was to her.

"This sounds ominous. Are you okay, Christa?"

She could hear Merihem weakening and his concern coming across. "I am, but… my blissful one isn't," she confessed.

"What. The. Fuck! Who? Does Dakata know? I knew it was catching. It's like an epidemic. First Dakata, then me, then Scott, now you!"

Oh, so she had been right about Scott! Good for him, he could do with a little shake up in his life. "Merihem, focus! Can you get me in to see the king?"

"Oh, fuck… it's Wanda, isn't it! No, don't tell me, shit! Fucksake. Alright, but you'll owe me!"

She grinned, her face raised to the sun, enjoying the warmth against her skin. "Thank you. And I need it to happen asap."

"You fucking would," he grumped. "Leave it with me. I'll get back in touch within the hour."

She said goodbye to herself because he'd already hung up on her. Christa continued on down towards the house barefooted. The closer she got, the easier it was to see the neglect. Bigger than Silas's home, and clearly built for a family, she walked around the outside, wondering why Wanda had done nothing with it. It had so much potential, not that she couldn't see the appeal of living in Wanda's trees. They moved to accommodate them, their needs.

Christa could admit that she missed her large bath, with water jets that could hit just the right spot. Cold water from the lake, though fresh and reinvigorating, wasn't quite the same as a hot bath. And what would it be like in winter? She shivered at the very idea of washing in icy water, despite what the humans believed about the benefits.

As for everything else the trees offered, the leaves made a very comfortable bed. She could conjure whatever food she felt like. Not one to watch TV often or be big on social media, Christa didn't miss them. She tried the door handle, surprised when it opened with ease. With a thought, she had sandals on her feet before stepping inside the musty smelling house.

The inside was worse than the outside. Mold grew up the walls, darkening the paint and wallpaper. Wood had started rotting, and the floorboards creaked ominously under her sandals. She flicked a light switch, and nothing happened. The taps in the kitchen produced just clunky metal grating noises. Yet the place was open and bright, where the light came in past the dirt on the windows. The place had potential.

Christa walked to the doors leading out into the orchard, and with a little shove, they opened to give her a perfect view of the orchard. She rearranged the house in her mind as she walked through, lost in her thoughts for so long, she jerked when her phone rang.

Seeing Merihem's name, she swiped the screen, putting him on speaker without the threat of interruption. "It's done. One of his staff will contact you with the date and time. Don't miss it. And whatever you do, don't mention Dakata's name."

She laughed at the absurdity of doing something so foolish. "Got it."

"Be careful, he's not in the best of moods."

She sobered at what that could mean for her, for Wanda. "Thank you," she murmured with complete sincerity.

"You're welcome. Just don't fuck up and land me back in trouble."

It had taken five days to get an audience with King Asmodeus and only after she had rung Merihem twice more to get things moving. Christa had a growing sense of urgency to talk about the next steps and didn't feel she could until they had dealt with protecting the forest.

Wanda's fear sometimes felt less, but it wasn't, not really. She loathed to move outside the orchard. Christa didn't need Wanda to say how she felt because, unwillingly, she shared it. Sometimes through her nightmares. In Christa's mind, the only way to remove that fear was to make the forest safe from all visitors. To give Wanda back her freedom to choose if going to the forest was something she wanted to do.

"I won't be long, I swear." Christa kissed Wanda, her lips soft and sweet, from the breakfast they'd shared, making her linger.

Wanda clung to her, desperation pouring off her.

"I have to go, or I'll be late." She hated the feeling growing inside her when Wanda attempted to smile, only her lips trembled. "I'll be fine. I have several leaves in my pocket. The girls have taken good care of me, so I'll be fine while we're apart." She'd discovered they had been sneaky at that first meeting and snuck leaves into her coat, and why she'd not suffered as Dakata had by the initial separation after Wanda's rejection.

Christa stroked the trunk of the nearest tree with affection. "They will keep you distracted while I am gone." She came closer and whispered in Wanda's ear, as she slipped a hand between her legs, stroking over her sex, "I'll want you wet and aroused, but you aren't to come until I get back."

Wanda moaned and shuddered against Christa as her arousal scented the warm air between them. "Hurry."

"I will, beloved." Christa didn't give herself a chance to change her mind and translocated to the demon realm. She didn't consider wasting time going to her family's home. She already felt a drain on her energy. Was this the effect of leaving Wanda and her trees? She had no doubt it was.

It had been mere seconds and already she was stroking the leaves in her pocket, striding through the palace. Directed by staff to where she needed to go, Christa didn't waver in her aim to get to the king as quickly as possible. Despite having never been inside the palace before, she found her way easily.

On time and in the right room, a very bored-looking demon sat at a desk. The place was as ornate and stuffy as she imagined it would be.

The demon didn't so much as give her more than a courtesy glance before waving a hand. "Sit over there. Someone will call you."

Having never requested such a meeting, she was clueless about what to expect, so Christa took the rather uncomfortable, hard leather seat and crossed her legs. Black silk trousers floated around her ankle as her foot, in six-inch killer heels, bounced impatiently. The nervousness roaming freely through her at how this was all going to turn out—if for some awful reason she failed—worsened with her not knowing how Wanda was coping in the forest without her. It was a necessity, because Wanda coming with her was an impossibility. Did it make a difference knowing that? Hell, no!

Whatever Christa had expected to feel, it wasn't this soul sucking weight that worsened with every second she was away from Wanda. Like an absolute eternity passing in every breath, or what she imagined it would be like. She hated it.

Had she become clingy? Was that even a thing with a blissful one?

Christa gave a mournful sigh and stared at the large, ornate door she was sitting outside, willing it to open.

She checked her wristwatch. How had it only been five minutes?

Was Wanda feeling the same anxiety?

Christa wished she wasn't when her own nagged like a toddler denied sweets.

In the demon realm, Christa had no sense of their connection, and she could not deny it made her antsy in ways she'd never truly experienced before. It didn't matter that she'd asked Dakata to keep an eye out for anything untoward. Or that she'd encouraged the trees to distract Wanda. Even that she'd sensed Dougal approaching Wanda's trees before she'd translocated to the demon realm. None of it mattered when she was here, and Wanda was *alone*.

Will you stop it? Christa snapped back at her demon.

I can't help it.

"The king is ready to see you."

Thank the demon gods!

Christa rose, not rolling her eyes at her dramatic other half, and walked on slightly unsteady legs towards the open door.

Show no weakness, her demon demanded.

Then you face him!

They'd argued over which side of them should speak and in the end, they had both decided if they wanted to play to Asmodeus's human side, then she needed to be in that form for this meeting.

Christa walked through the open door and met the gaze of the huge demon, whose nose wrinkled the moment the door closed behind her.

"You smell of m—the forest." He scowled and rose, coming closer, his eyes narrowing as Christa remained where she was, unsure if meeting him halfway was advisable.

He came to a stop, looking down his regal nose at her. "Why did you seek this meeting? Your brother isn't causing an issue in the forest, is he?" he growled menacingly.

Oh boy, thanks Dakata!

Chapter Seventeen

Wanda

Wanda wanted to be brave for Christa, she did. The first couple of minutes after Christa left, she listened to her trees, accepted the gentle encouragement to breathe.

Someone needed to talk to her lungs. They weren't behaving. The tight band that was currently crushing her chest made sucking in air impossible.

She will be fine, beloved. Breathe for us.

Leaves stroked up and down her bare arms and a sob escaped when it did no more than make the anxiety increase. Anxiety, the kind she had never experienced before—and after everything she had gone through in the demon realm, that was saying something—made her insides feel like they were being stretched, then hit repeatedly with something sharp. Her body vibrated with pain, hitting every nerve cell inside her.

Please, beloved, you need to focus on us.

The request made everything worse when Wanda felt she was betraying her trees because she couldn't obey. She wanted to. Wanted to do what Christa had insisted she should do and let her trees distract her. But she could no longer sense Christa. Their connection was… severed.

Another sob escaped as she clutched at branches, gasping for air. Her tears blinded her as they fell unheeded. They made her feel even more defenseless, so she curled into a ball, hiding from herself and from her own lack. Sobbing harder, her chest burned, her face buried in her knees, doing everything to keep hold of the distress and prevent her trees from suffering.

Her limbs grew heavy, and the world shrank, closing her into misery. The cradle of her trees as they swayed and rocked her made no difference to the feelings crushing her.

Images floated unbidden to the surface of her mind of what the demons had done to her. Panting, she squeezed her eyes tightly together.

Beloved, please breathe in our scent.

Wanda heard the words floating through her mind, but she wasn't able to grasp them, focus on them.

What if the demons choose to harm Christa? How would she know? She was useless, crippled by her own thoughts that she wouldn't be able to get Christa the help she needed.

"Lass, what is it?" Dougal's voice came through the branches like he was miles away, in a tunnel of trees. "I feel your distress. What has happened? How can I help?"

Wanda couldn't answer, couldn't concentrate on what he was saying. Leaves caressed her and with them came the scent of Christa. Wanda, greedy for more, released a body shaking breath and worked to suck in a breath to smell Christa. Her hands balled into her chest, willing it to work.

That's it, beloved, smell the leaves.

She reached blindly for them and brought them to her nose, mewling as she inhaled deeply, yearning them to turn into Christa.

Wanda didn't see the branches part, she felt it before the breeze touched her arms.

"Oh, lass, are you hurt?"

With a struggle, Wanda uncurled, lifting her head. She opened her eyes to look at Dougal. Her lips were working, but no sound came out, except for the whimpers of distress. "Hold on, lass. I'll go get Silas for you."

Would he understand? Be able to help her? Desperation made her nod wildly, curls flicking over the bed of leaves she lay on. Struggling as she was to just keep breathing, she didn't notice her trees expanding the surrounding space. Her eyes closed once more, so she didn't see Dougal running carelessly through the forest to get Silas.

Why did it hurt so much?

Was this being separated from Christa, or were her fears coming true?

She shuddered violently.

Was Christa hurt?

Dead?

Beloved, we would know if she was dead. Please stop these thoughts. Christa will be fine. We have protected her.

Not from the demons that might hurt her because of me.

Her thoughts tumbled from one disaster to another. She didn't notice the leaves wrapping themselves around her, working to stop her violent shivers. Misery tugged her into a dark place where there was no sunlight. Where the darkness had sharp claws and wanted to peel the skin from her body. From her soul.

Christa.

Christa.

Christa, come back to me.

Wanda rocked back and forth, her eyes unseeing as she stared out of her nook.

"Wanda. Wanda, I'm here." Silas's voice floated in the air, and she worked to catch it. Hear what he was saying. "Shush my love, I'm here."

Strong arms wrapped around her shuddering body. A familiar warmth pressed against hers and caused a broken sob. The scent of Silas made her twist and bury her head into his chest, tears flowing down her icy skin, seeking solace.

"Do you know what happened, Dougal?" Silas questioned quietly, stroking up and down Wanda's back.

"The wind encouraged me to pay Wanda a visit. When I got here, I felt her distress," Dougal answered. "The lass was beside herself. Even her trees couldn't help her."

"Christa has gone to the demon realm," she heard Dakata say as yet more shudders ran through her.

They had reasoned out the need for Christa to go, but Wanda could not think of one of them now. She wanted Christa here, safe in her arms.

"How do you know that?"

"Because she asked me to watch over Wanda while she was gone."

"You never said."

Was Silas hurt by this?

Wanda pressed closer to her brother, hating that she had somehow caused an issue between him and Dakata.

"It's fine, Wanda. I understand why Christa would do such a thing."

She didn't need to see his face to know he meant it, but it didn't help.

She lost the thread of the conversation that carried on around her as she drew strength from Silas. Their bond was so pure, his magic worked with that of her trees. The trees gathered around them, holding them both, helping to reduce Wanda's distress.

She had no concept of time as it passed. Her head felt too heavy to move along with her limbs, even when it became a little easier to get the air to go into her body.

Breath in.

Breath out.

Breath in.

Breath out.

She mentally repeated it with her trees.

"—go to the demon realm." She roused at Dakata's voice.

"If you feel that would be the wisest thing to do?" The strain was evident in Silas's voice as he tensed against her. Dakata had not been back to the demon realm since...

Her nose wrinkled at the familiar scent and with effort, Wanda opened her heavy-lidded, swollen eyes, releasing a cry.

"What... what happened here?" Christa's demon wore a lethal expression, her gaze sweeping the forest, hands raised, deadly looking claws ready to attack.

"You're back," Wanda whispered tearfully. This time, the tears came in a flood of relief.

Wobbly and weak, Wanda attempted to climb out of the tree to get to Christa, her need to touch driving her. However, after the panic attack, all she could do was crawl to the edge of the open nook.

Christa's demon was already reaching for her and effortlessly lifted her out to enfold her in her arms. Wanda's feet dangled three feet off the ground as she threaded her arms under Christa's hair and hugged her tightly, laying her cheek against Christa's.

"I'm sorry," she sobbed. "I wanted to be brave."

"Hush now, my love." Christa gently moved Wanda, one arm hooking under her bottom, holding her steady, while running her fingers down the side of Wanda's cheek, being careful with the claws. "I understand. You couldn't feel our connection. I should have considered that. But once I was there, I couldn't leave, I'm sorry."

"No," Wanda sobbed. "I—"

A finger pressed against Wanda's lips, stopping her from saying more. "It's okay. I'm safe. Unharmed. And I understand. I do. I won't leave you again, I swear."

"Did the demon king agree to your request?" Dakata asked, sounding concerned.

"What request is this?" Dougal's usual affable nature seemed to have disappeared. The gruff demand was anything but friendly.

"To protect the forest from demons and unwelcome visitors intending to harm," Christa answered, as Wanda felt exhaustion creeping through her at the release of tension and anxiety. "I need Wanda to feel safe in her own home once more."

"Aye, I can see why you would want that. Did the king agree?"

Wanda moved so she could see Dougal's face. She sensed something was amiss, but his expression gave her no clue as to what it was. She would speak to him alone when she felt more like herself.

"He has and is planning to come tomorrow." A flood of absolute relief came from Christa as she spoke.

"He will?" Dakata questioned, his shocked expression very easy to read. "Do you have to do anything for this?"

Wanda, who had relaxed, instantly tensed at Dakata's question. "Did he want something for it?" she asked before Christa could answer her brother.

Christa met Wanda's gaze. Giving her a reassuring smile. "No. His only request was to meet you."

"What? Me?" Wanda squeaked in alarm. "Why does he want to meet me?" It was hard enough with Dakata, and the others she sensed that came and went, who Christa said were good. The idea of meeting the most powerful demon left her dry mouthed and terrified.

A gentle finger touched the wrinkled skin at the bridge of her nose. "Because you are my blissful one. He won't harm you, he is just intrigued."

"Oh…"

Chapter Eighteen

Christa

Christa got the sense that Dougal wasn't too happy about what was going on in his forest, yet when she'd invited him to meet King Asmodeus to allay any worries he had about the magic the king would use, he had politely declined.

He'd ambled off, leaving Silas and Dakata, grumbling something under his breath that Christa hadn't quite caught. Because what she thought she heard made little sense.

"Why can't he see it's all the same?"

Same as what, she didn't know and wasn't concerned with when Wanda wouldn't let go of her. Admittedly, Christa's demon didn't want to let go either, with the memory of how distressed Wanda was when they had translocated back into the forest as soon as her meeting was over.

Christa suspected Wanda had been much worse with how she had clutched at Silas, and the relief Dakata had not concealed at seeing her. She would need to check in with the trees too, as she had picked up on their unease.

"What's wrong with Dougal?" Silas murmured, his gaze looking in the direction that Dougal had disappeared.

"I should imagine we blindsided him by bringing a demon king into the forest to protect it."

Silas looked thoughtful. "Do you think so?"

Christa had no clue. She didn't know the troll that well to make any suggestions. Wanda hadn't raised a concern about asking the demon king to the forest and she knew Dougal well enough to have mentioned it, if it would be an issue. Wouldn't she?

"What is worrying you?" Dakata slipped an arm around Silas, kissing his temple.

"I sense something." Silas shook his head. "I'll speak to him."

Christa smiled at them both, not wanting to be rude and asking them to leave after supporting Wanda, but… "Thank you for looking after Wanda."

Silas inclined his head, an ethereal smile forming that made her brother look at his blissful one with a smitten expression that got Christa struggling to contain her amusement.

"You're both welcome, and it was no trouble when I got to spend some time with my sister."

Wanda blushed a bright shade of red.

"We've been a little busy getting to know each other," Christa supplied, wanting to take the pressure off Wanda when she clutched a little tighter to her, distress coming through their bond. "We'll come and pay you a visit once the demon king protects the forest," Christa promised.

He reached up and tugged gently on one of Wanda's curls. "I'll look forward to it." He came up on his toes to press a kiss to Wanda's cheek.

Dakata came and took hold of Silas's hand. "I'm sure you want to be left alone now." He looked directly at Christa as she nodded. "If you need anything, just let us know."

"I will and again, thank you."

They didn't linger any longer and followed the direction Dougal had taken. Wanda ran her nose down the side of Christa's neck, her breath tickling the skin as she inhaled deeply. "I need you," she murmured.

"You have me, my love." Once within reaching distance of their trees, branches formed steps within the nook. Christa carried Wanda inside, the trees remaining quiet. They kept their distance, giving Christa reason to pause.

Blocking Wanda, she reached out to the girls. *I sense something is wrong.*

We couldn't console her. Her fear for you was too great. It consumed her.

Christa felt the clutch in her belly at their concern and how they would have lived that pain and fear with Wanda. *I'm sorry.*

No, beloved, you have nothing to be sorry for. It's just... we have never failed her before.

You didn't fail her. I felt the loss of our connection, as I'm sure you did, too. I miscalculated her fear. So I'm sorry for the distress I caused you all.

It was necessary for you to go. We know this. Protecting the forest and Wanda is vital to everyone's survival. Christa felt their sadness. *It means leaving us will be… difficult.*

I won't leave again, I promise.

You can't promise this.

I can and I am. Her demon spoke for both of them. They could protect the forest, and initially Christa thought that would be enough to remove Wanda's fear. This conversation proved her wrong. Wanda might never be ready for Christa to leave her and go to the demon realm. As she lowered the tree fairy down on the lush bed of leaves, the feelings she held for Wanda—for her trees—meant that offering this promise was the easiest thing she'd ever done.

"We'll never leave you again, love."

The leaves rustled and branches laden with fruit swayed in approval. Wanda's mouth formed a perfect O as her gaze held Christa's.

"I-I… really?"

Christa's demon receded, her clothes disappearing as she kneeled down next to Wanda. The branches closed around them to conceal them. "Yes. I am yours and you are mine, along with your girls. I don't have any needs beyond this orchard."

It was the utter truth. Christa would talk about the neglected house some other time. For now, she wanted to give Wanda what she desired.

She brushed a kiss over Wanda's soft, parted lips. "Lift your arms," she requested in a whisper. "Let me love you."

Wanda remained flushed, tears still stained her cheeks, and her eyes were puffy, but none of it distracted from her allure as a shy smile appeared when she lifted her arms.

Christa ran her fingers down from Wanda's wrists, caressing the silky skin. Holding her gaze, Christa expressed how much she loved when Wanda offered herself in this way. She witnessed her breath hitch, and her pupils dilate as Christa caressed the sides of her breast as she magically removed the dress covering Wanda's ample curves.

Pale, silky skin glowed with vitality. Her nipples hardened under Christa's proprietary stare. "Look at you. So stunning. You take my breath away." Christa ran the tip of her finger over one pink bud. "Spread your legs for me. Show me how much you want me."

Wanda's moan was low and breathy. Her thighs parting caused a tug of arousal at Christa's core. Ignoring it, she knelt between Wanda's legs, coming forward to suck a nipple into her mouth, her hair cascading over Wanda's body. Using her tongue, Christa bathed the firm bud, feeling it tighten. She teased the tip while taking the other bud and squeezing it, rolling it between the tips of her fingers before tugging on it until Wanda was gasping, her full breasts heaving from the caress.

Christa scented Wanda's increasing arousal. Cupping both breasts, she gently kneaded the flushed, warm skin, then switched between each nipple. Licking, sucking and teasing the tightening buds as they darkened with desire. She listened to every whimper, cry, and moan as Wanda shivered, her body pressing closer to Christa's, her inner thighs rubbing against Christa's.

"I can smell your arousal. Are you wet, my love?" Christa murmured, letting go and getting a moan of complaint. Her eyes roamed down over Wanda's soft, full, flushed curves.

"Yes… please touch me." Her eyes implored Christa as her thighs quivered and bore the proof of her desire.

A wicked gleam appeared in Christa's eyes. "Let me worship you like the beautiful pillow princess you are."

Wanda squirmed as she complied, and Christa's breath caught at the gorgeous picture she made. Cascading curls fanned around her flushed face. They gleamed in the soft flickering sunlight that came through the overhead canopy, which dappled her skin with beams of light. Wanda stretched her arms above her head, revealing every abundant inch of her. Cream, plump thighs moved restlessly against the lush bed beneath her. Wanda's sex was flushed with arousal and slick with the evidence of her desire. Christa's body reacted to the sight, but she didn't want to rush. She wanted to torment them both for as long as possible.

Producing a bottle of warming oil with a thought, she gave Wanda all of her attention. Flicking the cap open, she trickled the fragrant oil over her breasts. Moans poured from Wanda's lips as it slid over the sides and down the valley of her breasts where it pooled. Setting the bottle aside, Christa followed the path of the oil, groaning with Wanda at the warm, slippery feeling.

"So good," Wanda whimpered, her skin quivering at Christa's slow, sensual, gliding hands.

Up and over her breasts, down the valley to her round belly, her hands parted to go down the silky thighs. Christa spread the oil, her fingers grazing the crease of Wanda's groin, temptingly close, only to move away and tease them both.

She rubbed oil over every inch of Wanda's body in slow and sensual glides, her fingers pressing firmly, then lightening the touch until Wanda was begging for more.

Her hips lifted rhythmically when Christa ran her fingers temptingly close to her sex.

"Please… please… touch me." She punctured each word with a keen of desire. Her belly trembled and her arousal thickened the air. Thighs pressing closer, Wanda never once reached to touch herself. She waited for Christa.

"I am, my love." Christa ran her hands up the insides of Wanda's legs, her oily fingers stroking down both sides of her sex, opening her. Christa held Wanda's gaze and licked her lips. "Do you want my tongue? My fingers? Or my clit against yours?"

Wanda's whole body shivered, and Christa delighted in the effect she had on Wanda. "Clit," she gasped. "Your clit on mine."

Christa gulped in heavily scented air, working to control her desire as she lifted one of Wanda's legs to slip her knee under her buttock, bringing their bodies closer together. The oil aided in the move and got a barrage of sensual sounds pouring from Wanda's parted lips.

Holding Wanda's leg outstretched over the thigh under her, Christa rose and slipped her other leg over the top of Wanda, placing her knee down next to her hip. Coming across Wanda's body at an angle, Christa could feel the heat from Wanda's sex. Breathless with desire, she maneuvered Wanda until their legs scissored to allow Christa to grind against Wanda's clit with her own.

"Ohhhh," Wanda cried out at the sensual rub of oil, desire and skin on skin contact which also left Christa ready to spiral out of control into a world of bliss. She opened herself to feel Wanda's pleasure and then fed back her own.

Christa sucked in a breath, released it, and inhaled the sex scented air again, defying her own need in an attempt to keep control until Wanda fell apart.

Wanda's heavy-lidded gaze never left her, adding to Christa's need to give her everything she desired. As aroused as Christa, the heat and scent from Wanda's sex became more intoxicating with each breath.

Christa rolled into her, fucking her clit against Wanda's, soaking in every whimper and cry. "That's it, my love, let me hear you. Let me hear how much you want me to fuck you."

Her body jerked against Christa's as Wanda came, her whole body arched up, hung suspended as come soaked Christa, and triggered her own orgasm. It railroaded her as she clung to Wanda, the tremors of pleasure stealing her breath.

How long her body shook with the aftereffects, Christa had no idea, but her skin had cooled, and she could no longer support herself with her trembling limbs. Carefully moving back, Christa lay down at Wanda's side, then, using the last of her energy, lifted Wanda on top of her.

She tucked Wanda's curls behind her ear, exposing flushed skin and a serene expression. *You are my world.* Christa kissed the tip of Wanda's nose as her eyelids fluttered open. "Sleep, I'll watch over you."

Wanda curled a hand into Christa's hair and tucked her face into her neck in a move that flooded Christa with so many emotions. "I know, beloved," she slurred, her eyes closing, "you are my world, too."

Chapter Nineteen

Wanda

Wanda woke early, heavy-limbed, and with a wonderful sense of contentment running through her. For a moment, she could almost believe that her panic attack had never happened. Only it had, and Christa had made a promise to Wanda. Did she really mean it?

Wanda, now without her thoughts clouded with desire, couldn't see how Christa could make such a promise. To look at the woman sleeping beside, her arm wrapped around Wanda's waist as they lay facing each other, she didn't doubt that Christa had meant it, at the time. The hours Christa had spent cherishing every inch of her until she'd lost count of how many times she'd brought her to climax, was about making her forget. And for a short time, Wanda had.

She spoke the truth. The whisper from her trees drew her attention.

I know she believes it.

But you do not?

Wanda sighed at the feeling of disappointment that came from her girls. *I want to, but she has a life beyond the forest. A family in the demon realm she will wish to see. To spend time with.*

They will come here.

Wanda's heart leapt at the possibility of that. *Is it that simple? I… I would not want anyone else to come inside my trees.*

It can be simple. You have a home close by.

Wanda frowned and considered if that was an actual option. *It is derelict.*

Christa has the power to change that.

"Your mind is very busy this morning, my love," Christa murmured sleepily.

So focused on the trees, she hadn't noticed Christa watching her. "I didn't mean to wake you."

Christa kissed her softly, the hint of peach sweetness lingered from the meal they'd eaten before falling asleep. "I don't mind." She nuzzled along her jaw to her ear, a hand pushing the hair away to reveal the sensitive skin behind it. She placed a kiss on her madly beating pulse. "Talk to me."

Wanda sighed in pleasure at the tongue stroking over her skin and struggled to think. "I don't know... how you can keep your promise."

The tongue disappeared, and Christa pulled back to give Wanda a look that came with a feeling that Wanda didn't know how to interrupt. "I would never make a promise I could not keep."

Hurt.

She had hurt Christa with her lack of faith. Yet Wanda couldn't just set aside the reality of such a promise. "I believe you." She ran her fingers over Christa's cheek. The softness of her skin belied the warrior inside. *My warrior.* "But you have a family in the demon realm, friends I expect, too. I can't ask you to—"

"Wanda, you don't need to ask. We can build a life here. Together." Christa's hand came up and cupped the back of Wanda's. "I was going to talk to you about the—"

"House," Wanda finished, her lips quirking up, suspecting her trees had picked up Christa's intentions to talk about the house and fed them to her on purpose.

"Yes. I went down through the orchard to look at it. I wanted to see what was inside."

Her brows arched in wonder. "You did? When?" Wanda had no recollection of Christa leaving her alone.

"Yes, a few days back while you were sleeping one morning. I could see you the whole time, my love, and your trees kept watch for me, too." There was hope coming from Christa and Wanda clung to it. Clung to the idea that whatever was coming, they would find a middle ground. "It's got so much potential."

The house was rotting away from neglect. "Potential? What do you mean?"

"With a little bit of love and a big dose of magic, we can return the house to its original state. We could also move the house closer to your trees, like Silas's. Or leave it where it is," Christa rushed on to say, most definitely picking up Wanda's dislike of the house encroaching on her trees.

What if Christa chose the house over their trees? "Do you want to live in the house?" Wanda had never lived in one before and she wasn't sure she wanted to, even for Christa. She wasn't like Silas.

You must not be selfish, beloved.

I don't want to be.

Then wait for Christa to explain.

"I love our trees,"—she cast her arm up—"and being this close to them."

Wanda knew Christa spoke the truth, and it eased the knots of tension gathering in her stomach. However, she sensed the 'but', even though Christa said nothing more. "Yet, you would like some aspects of living in a house?"

She watched Christa closely, seeing a moment of indecision before she nodded. "I would love a proper bathroom. Hot water to soak in. Scented bubbles. I love the lake, but nothing beats a hot bath to ease one's soul."

It was not what Wanda expected, and a giggle escaped at the answer. "A bathroom. Is that it?"

Christa pressed her lips softly against Wanda's. "Yes. I have everything else here with you. If we had the house repaired, then family and friends, whom you rightly pointed out I'd want to see, could come to the house, keeping our trees just for us."

The surrounding rustling suggested the trees approved of this idea, too.

Christa grinned. "It looks like our girls approve. So what do you say, my love?"

"I've never had a bubble bath."

Christa's laughter shook her body as she brought Wanda closer, their naked skin sliding against each other, the residual oil making Wanda tingle between her thighs. "Then that will be the first thing we do once the king has protected the forest for us and the house is restored."

Not having forgotten about the visit, Wanda had worked not to dwell on it with so much else to think about. Left with no choice now, she sighed heavily.

"When will he arrive?" She wanted what he offered, she just wasn't sure what to expect. What to imagine he would be like. He wanted to meet her, but she wasn't sure if the meeting would include Christa.

"Later this morning. I will know when he decides to come." Christa claimed her mouth in a soul searing kiss that left her wanting more. They rolled on the bed of soft leaves until Wanda lay beneath Christa, limbs entangled, mouths never parting. Wrapped in each other's arms as they were left Wanda unable to think when all she could do was feel. Feel the love Christa gave willingly. The love of her warrior.

"Yes, my love. A warrior for you, always."

Her dress was simple. Peach with cream trim around the arms and across the bodice, that she tugged at it, looking down at the hint of exposed cleavage. Wanda wondered if it was too revealing. She didn't have any other that differed in style. She huffed out a breath, glancing at her bare feet which peeped out from the bottom of the hem of her dress. Should she have shoes on?

"You look beautiful," said Christa, as she returned to their trees. She had gone outside minutes ago to make sure they were ready for the king. Ready how, Wanda had no clue. She stood at the entrance of their nook, looking stunning in a forest green silk dress and black, six-inch heels, in her demon form.

There was Wanda's warrior. Red skin gleamed in the sunlight, as did the silver tips of her horns. Inky black hair flowed over her breasts, reaching her waist.

Christa, in either form, was clearly biased. "Should I put on shoes?"

She squeaked aloud as Christa plucked her out of the tree and kissed her. They had not long bathed and eaten after Christa had kept her occupied using her very talented mouth and hands. "You are perfect as you are."

"It seems you are as smitten as your brother," rumbled a deep, menacing voice behind them.

Wanda's heart slammed against her chest, fear prickling her skin at the sound as she forced herself to glance over her shoulder. The air caught in her throat at the huge demon wearing an expression that chilled Wanda. The attire was more casual than Wanda expected of a king. Dark trousers and shirt covered a massive chest, bulging muscles and powerful thighs.

Wanda gulped in fright. Christa was tall, even in heels, but the king towered over them by at least another foot-and-a-half.

Christa didn't seem intimidated as she lowered Wanda to the forest floor, thankfully keeping her right next to her side. "She is my blissful one. My beloved."

The king turned his attention to Wanda as he stepped closer, moving silently. His thick, black brows drew together, his full lips pursing. "You are... such a small thing."

The trees behind her stroked down her back, giving her courage. "I'm a dryad. None of our kind are big."

Offer him a drink.

You think that's wise?

Yes.

Listening to the trees, she bravely took a step towards the giant. "Would you like a glass of peach juice?"

The king's gaze shifted to her trees, and Wanda heard them waving as branches clicked together, witnessing the king's amusement. "Your trees are…"

"Saying hello. My girls are friendly." They were with those they trusted. And Wanda took solace from that. She trusted Christa implicitly, but her bond with her trees had formed many years ago.

He didn't reply, and he wore an intrigued expression as he walked past Wanda. Christa clutched her a little tighter as they turned to watch the king stop at the closest tree. He easily reached up and plucked one of the peaches he was offered. He brought it to his nose, but Wanda couldn't see his face to figure out what he thought about the gift.

Seconds ticked by and Wanda wasn't sure what to make of the fact her trees had shut her out or that Christa chuckled and the king continued to stand looking up at her girls. Was he talking with them?

A moment later, he swung around, holding a glass of juice in his other hand. "Would you like to take a seat?" Wanda enquired like a good host.

He motioned for Christa and Wanda to lead the way. Wanda walked to the old fallen tree they used as a seat. One look at it and Wanda could see it would not accommodate the king's bulk. Then a large wooden seat appeared, and Wanda wasn't sure if it was Christa or the king who had materialized it. He took it and Christa guided Wanda to the log.

Sitting, Christa reached for Wanda's clammy hand and squeezed it gently, giving her a reassuring smile.

"Leave us Christa."

Wanda started at the command, her fingers tightening around Christa's.

Chapter Twenty

Christa

Christa felt that hateful wave of fear from her blissful one once more. It was strong enough to make her shake her head and defy the king, despite the possible consequences.

"I'm not leaving Wanda." She added as much force to make her point without being rude.

His eyes revealed exactly what he thought of her denial as she held his gaze, never wavering. She ignored the clutch in her belly, having promised Wanda to protect her no matter what.

"Is that so?" There was zero infliction in the king's voice, giving nothing away, but it still caused a shiver to run through her.

She swallowed hard, her throat clicking. "Wanda does not cope with being left alone in a demon's company *after the attack and kidnapping*." She gave him her best winning smile, pushed on by her human side. "I'm sure you understand that causing my blissful one distress is something I would never do intentionally. Leaving her would be an intentional act."

A flicker of what looked like pain came and went over his stern features. Confused, Christa searched his expression, going over what she said, looking for what could cause such a reaction.

She came up blank as his lips thinned in obvious displeasure. She felt the atmosphere crackle with the strain of not bowing to his wish, but not once did she shift her attention to Wanda like she wanted to.

"I'll be—"

The king held up the hand still holding the peach and stopped Wanda from whatever she'd been about to say. "She can stay."

"Thank you," Wanda murmured, her grip finally relaxing, though the tension in the body pressed close to Christa's never eased.

Christa knew this was a big win, given the king's reputation and lack of tolerance for those disobeying his orders, so she acknowledged it.

Bowing her head, she said, "King Asmodeus, I'm grateful for your understanding."

He never acknowledged Christa and kept staring at Wanda. "When did you know Christa belonged to you? How did you feel?"

Huh?

What kind of questions were these? They taught a demon to recognize their blissful one in their soul.

"I'm not sure what you mean?" Wanda looked at Christa frowning, eyes full of worry. "Belong?"

"Yes, belong. I speak perfect English," he snapped. The sigh that followed when Wanda winced at his tone was unexpected, as was his apology, which left Christa slack jawed.

"I apologize. We are taught about Blissful Ones as young demons. Yet I have no recollection of ever meeting a couple who had—have such a connection until Dakata... then Merihem and Peni."

"I can see how that would give you some concern," Wanda replied softly. "I only knew of such a connection before Christa, because of my brother. He felt an attraction to Dakata upon sight and became intrigued."

"Intrigued? How so?" King Asmodeus came forward in his seat, making it creak. The glass he held appeared forgotten as the juice swished dangerously close to the rim.

Wanda rubbed a knuckle over her eyebrow, pushing back her tumbling curls. "He couldn't stop thinking about Dakata after he saw him."

"Was it the same for you?"

Christa now found herself fascinated by the many emotions she could see as Wanda nibbled on her lower lip, looking down at their joined hands. "I have no recollection of seeing Christa in the demon realm."

Was she hedging?

"I see." Asmodeus brought the glass to his lips, sipping. His eyes widened as he looked at what he held. "Why, it's delicious."

Wanda giggled when her trees made sure to let the king know they were pleased he liked it.

Looking back towards the trees, the king's long hair shifted around his shoulders like a black silk cape. The girls swayed and Christa caught Wanda's eye roll before the king returned his attention to them. "So when you did meet, what did you feel?" he asked, clearly not letting the subject drop.

"The first time Christa came to the forest to see if I was alright, something about her tugged at…" she blushed, plucking at the fabric of her dress, once more not looking directly at anyone. "She touched me, and I felt"—her brow furrowed—"alive."

"Alive. How?"

Her slim shoulders shrugged. "My soul, it connected to Christa's, even when my head was terrified of what it meant with Christa being a demon and what happened in your realm."

"What changed?" Wanda held all of Asmodeus's attention.

Her lips formed a wobbly smile. "Dougal, a troll who lives in the forest, is a dear friend. Between him and my trees, they explained Christa would never harm me." She sighed and lay her head on Christa's arm, regret lodging in her stomach. "I knew it, deep down, but my fear wouldn't let me acknowledge it. I spoke with Silas, too, trying to make sense of it all."

Asmodeus's eyes narrowed, his chest moving rapidly. "Have you?"

"Made sense of it?" she questioned, and he nodded. "I don't think we're meant to make sense of it."

He could not deny the honesty in her words, yet Christa could see the skepticism in the sneer. "How can that be so? To determine the world around us, we must be able to make sense of things. Reason them out."

Wanda shook her head. "No, I don't believe that when it comes to bonds like this. Fate, they decide if someone should receive the gift of a mate—blissful one. How can we apply logic to this when there is no reasoning as to who gets such a gift? And it is a gift, one our souls recognize and accept with no need for any clarification. It just is. Logic comes from the mind and not the heart and soul. How can we apply it to something that has no logic at all?"

King Asmodeus's lips parted, closed, parted, then closed again. His dark eyes swirled with so many emotions that Christa found it difficult to take a breath waiting for him to respond, when clearly he didn't like, or perhaps understand, what Wanda had said.

Christa understood. Accepted it. Wanted it with all of her being. It didn't need to be justified when Wanda now wanted what they shared.

He brought the glass to his lips and drained it, then it disappeared a moment later along with the peach he'd held before he stood. Wanda's brows arched as she leaned back when the king towered over her.

"I'll protect the forest and surrounding lands, you'll have nothing else to fear, Wanda. No being, human or otherwise, with malicious intent will get past my wards. You have my word on this." He gave a curt nod.

Christa became confused by the sudden change in topic and the mask of indifference Asmodeus now wore.

"Do you need anything from… me?" Wanda asked bravely, her hand trembling in Christa's.

"No, it is already done."

"How do we know it'll work?"

Christa braced, wary of how the king could perceive Wanda's question as a challenge to his ability.

His laughter, so unexpected, came with a smile that revealed a handsome man, and left Christa gawping. "You have nothing to fear, tree fairy. The wards will persuade those who wish to venture here to go elsewhere. They will also detect those with thoughts and intentions to cause harm. Those individuals will suffer pain, the likes they cannot comprehend, if they attempt to enter this forest. Anyone with an invite and with pure intentions will gain access without issue. Those you will know about because my wards will alert Christa of their presence. Does this answer your concerns? Fears?"

It wasn't any one thing, but Christa felt the weight of the invisible blanket of Wanda's fear lift at what Asmodeus promised her. She let go of Christa's hand and rose, taking the few steps to the king. Christa was up and right behind her, just in case.

She placed her trust in her blissful one to handle whatever her intentions were. That didn't mean she wasn't prepared to snatch Wanda away from the king if things became a problem for Wanda.

Dwarfed next to Asmodeus, Wanda had to stretch her head back at an awkward angle. "Saying thank you seems so little after what you have given me."

She opened her hand and there, on her palm, lay a rooted branch with a few lush, green leaves.

"I offer you this as a gift from my trees. If you plant it and look after it, you will have the deliciousness of fresh peaches whenever you wish. And a little part of the forest to remember what you have protected."

The sweetness of the gesture gave Christa's heart a little bump. She was also very curious about the king's cheeks, which looked to darken as he stared at the offered gift.

"That is very…" he met Wanda's stare and back was the smile, shocking Christa once more, "generous of you."

He took the offered gift, hesitated, then patted Wanda on the shoulder. The plant disappeared from his hand and became replaced by a small tumbling stone of blood red. It lay in the center of his palm, glowing in the sunlight. "A gift for you."

Wanda looked at the stone, then up at the king, frowning. "But you've already given me a gift."

He wore a look of impatience as he huffed. "Take it. You need only to rub your fingers over the surface three times and it will summon me… if there should ever be a need."

He was most definitely blushing. Christa would bet her life on it as she was back to being slack jawed at the gift. One that meant Wanda need never worry about being scared again, because she had the protection of Christa's king.

Her heart slammed against her ribs at the generosity of such a gesture. Never had she heard of him ever being this kind.

Wanda took it and bowed her head. "I will treasure it and hope I never need to use it."

The king's returning nod was curt, then he disappeared along with the chair he'd used.

Wanda looked about, then at the stone, before smiling at Christa. "That was… interesting."

That was one word for it! Christa wasn't sure she'd ever recover from the shock. "It was most certainly that. I do not believe he has ever offered a stone of such value to another soul. And the questions, I'm sure he never asked those of Dakata."

"Really?"

Christa gave it some thought, then shrugged, doing her best not to think too hard on the reasoning behind such magnanimous actions. Slipping an arm around Wanda's shoulders, needing the contact, she brushed a kiss over her forehead. "How about a trip to see Silas and Dakata to ask?"

Wanda gave her a searching look. "Is this a test?"

Was it? "Did I not feel you release the fear, my love?"

"I..." Wanda hesitated and leaned into Christa's touch, seeking comfort. "I did... it's just, I thought maybe we would take a walk to the house first... talk about what you feel needs to be done there? What you think would work for visitors?"

Warmth of the love they shared flooded Christa's chest and her demon receded. The size difference was still very noticeable, but Christa didn't need to bend as far when she wanted to kiss the upturned mouth.

Joy at all the possibilities effervesced inside her. "I think that's a perfect idea."

Chapter Twenty-One

Wanda

Christa was right, the fear had abated in a very noticeable way with the stone the demon gave her, but Wanda wasn't sure if she trusted its sudden disappearance. She knew what magic felt like and she suspected, but couldn't say for sure, that King Asmodeus had taken away her fear. If he had, she was grateful for it, but that didn't mean she wasn't wary, for now, of its return.

Tucking the stone into the bodice of her dress to prevent her rubbing at the surface accidentally, the presence of it lightened her heart. Except there was little time to focus on that when Christa took her hand to tug on it, encouraging her to walk with her or get dragged towards the house. Her enthusiasm was evident in every hurried step she took, even in high heels.

Wanda didn't understand why Christa chose to wear them, though she definitely appreciated how they made her legs look. The sexy line of her very long legs became accentuated. Curvy thighs led to shapely calves and slim ankles. The dress sat just below the knee. The silk clung to her voluptuous bottom and Wanda had an urge to walk behind so she could watch it sway.

"Don't you want to go?" Christa questioned, making Wanda take notice of the fact she'd slowed down and was working on catching a glimpse of Christa's backside.

Heat, which she totally blamed on the sun in the sky, filled her cheeks. "No... I mean yes." She groaned at her own silliness when her mind had wandered.

Christa searched her expression, and the light that appeared in her eyes made another part of Wanda heat. Pure wickedness. "Whatever has distracted you, my love?"

"I-I..." Wanda shook her head in frustration. "You, and how you look in heels and that silk skirt."

A slender brow arched, her lips quivering. "Is that so?"

"Yes, now shall we go?" She didn't give a laughing Christa a chance to reply and stomped past her. The grass beneath the soles of her feet had been warmed by the sun. Wanda concentrated on not standing on anything that might stab at the sole of her foot, choosing to ignore the demon continuing to laugh as she followed behind.

The lushness of her orchard made the house look even more neglected as she drew closer, and for the first time Wanda was sorry that she'd done nothing to nurture the home. It had love inside. She had felt it from the previous occupants the first time she had gone inside. The same love she'd felt from within the trees, and though neglected after those who owned the house died, it remained. A mainstay, keeping the trees alive, though not flourishing as they were now. She had nurtured that love by sharing her gift with them once they had accepted her.

As she walked up the rickety porch steps, it saddened her now that she had not done the same here.

"I can feel your sadness." Christa stopped inside the house's entrance. "We don't have to do this."

"I'm sad because I neglected the house." She let go of Christa's hand, walking over the dusty floors to touch the woodwork that someone had lovingly carved to create a staircase. The wood was rotting in places, coated in dirt and grime, and lacked the luster it must have once held. "Those who lived here built this home for their family. They loved this place." She turned to face Christa, who remained where she was. "I feel it."

"How about we add our own love to this place?" Christa's eyes held excitement as she walked carefully through the large room towards big, dirty windows. Before she had come to a stop, the windows sparkled and there was a view of Wanda's girls.

Christa looked back over her shoulders, grinning. "What do you think?"

"Would you want to live here?" Wanda asked again, keeping her emotions to herself. She could see the appeal for someone who had only ever lived inside a place like this.

Christa whirled around to face her, black silky strands catching in the beams of sunlight as they whipped out around her. Her head was already shaking before she'd come to a standstill. "I meant what I said Wanda. I would never lie to you."

She held Christa's intent look, walking towards her. "I know this." She took hold of Christa's hands, fingers threading together, trying to find the right words. "That doesn't mean you wouldn't or couldn't change your mind. I would understand. You have lived your whole life inside a house, a home. It's a lot to expect that you would not miss those comforts."

Christa brought her closer, their size difference meaning Wanda had to tilt her head back to hold her gaze. "What are those comforts compared to what I have with you? With our girls? You all give me everything I never knew I wanted or needed." She brought their joined hands up and kissed the knuckles of both hands. "My love, within your trees I have a sanctuary I would not exchange for a palace."

The same honesty as when she'd first asked was there. "If you ever change your mind, will you tell me?"

"Of course. I believe that won't happen."

To Wanda, Christa was the one sacrificing a life she had once known, and despite the ease with which Christa was willing to give that up, Wanda wanted Christa to know that she would try to live in the house if that time came. "But if it did, I would try."

Christa's hands slipped under Wanda's bottom and lifted her off the floor to claim Wanda's mouth in a fervent kiss. A kiss that left her breathless and distracted when Christa stopped moments later to speak. "Thank you for the offer, and I will keep that in mind if I should ever change my mind."

Wanda struggled to concentrate with the heat pooling between her thighs and the scent of Christa surrounding her. "Change your mind?" she asked, trying to get any remaining brain cells to function.

"My love, you flatter a girl in the best possible way." She kissed her again and Wanda gave up trying to figure out what Christa was referring to.

Christa encouraged her to wrap her legs around her waist as her dress disappeared, along with Christa's clothes. The evidence of her desire pressed against Christa's bare mound, and they both groaned. "This place is dirty," she murmured between kisses, making a mockery of what she was saying when she wasn't stopping.

"Not anymore," Christa replied after she stopped kissing her long enough for Wanda to focus.

Wanda blinked the room into focus and gasped at the change. Wood glowed with vitality, repaired and returned to its original glory. Furniture filled the space. A large, comfortable looking couch sat in front of the window. Matching, plump-cushioned chairs in forest green sat on either side of a fireplace that for a moment Wanda could envision holding a fire in the winter.

A large mahogany table sat in the room's corner, with seating for eight. Lamps sat on small tables at each end of the couch and one by each chair. A deep red rug covered most of the floor. Thick and plush looking, Wanda had an urge to sink her toes into it.

Wanda looked at Christa. "It's beautiful."

"The house I have in this realm looks like this, just without the view of our girls."

"What does your bathroom look like? The one you mentioned you enjoy using instead of my lake?"

Christa kissed the side of her mouth, nibbling on her full lower lip, sucking it between her teeth before releasing it. Her eyes sparkling with desire. "Let me show you."

In a blink, they were in a bathroom upstairs. Wanda struggled to catch her breath at translocating. Her memory of the previous occasions didn't surface, for which she was glad when Christa wore a look of expectation. "What do you think?"

Wanda took her time to pay attention to the room that had looked nothing like what it did now. First, it was in the wrong place. It was at the back of the house. The window it had was small, with frosted glass so no one could see out or in. The bath had brown stains up the sides, nearly reaching the lip, and the shower had dangled from a broken hook over it. Wanda did not wish to recall the state of the toilet or the ripped flooring with odd marks on it.

"It's stunning." It was. Large glass doors opened up onto the upper level porch facing directly over the trees. A large bathtub sat on polished wooden flooring before the doors, so a person could lie in the water and look out with an unfettered view.

Blue, red, orange and white tiles covered the walls in patterns that made no sense but looked pretty. A huge shower stall sat in the far corner, sun glinting off the chrome. A pristine white toilet sat next to it. On the other wall was a double basin within a marble countertop. The cabinet beneath had no door and Wanda counted no less than ten thick navy towels stacked in neat piles. On the counter by the sinks sat what appeared to be fifty or so bottles, in all shapes and sizes, with mysterious liquids inside in differing colors.

"Do you like to collect the bottles?"

The laugh sounded a little nervous. "I suppose. I like delightful smells when I bathe and can't resist when I find a new one to try."

Wanda giggled, endeared by this side of Christa. "Which is your favorite?" she asked, intrigued.

"Peaches."

Her giggles turned to laughter at Christa's quick response. "I'm sure it is." Pleased, despite herself, she nodded in the direction of the over laden counter. "Which of those is your favorite?"

Cheeks a rosy pink, Christa didn't put her down as she walked towards the counter. She paused and then the room became scented with the sweetness of cherry blossom.

"How?" Wanda twisted to look back at the source of the smell, her eyes widening at the full bath, topped with scented bubbles. "That looks very inviting," she admitted honestly.

"Want to try it out with me?"

Not looking away from the bath, she asked, "How do we do that? Will it be big enough for both of us?"

Moving towards it, Christa stepped into the water. Carefully, she lowered them both into the hot scented water, barely creating a ripple.

"Ohhhhhh," Wanda groaned at such decadence when the silkiness of the water caressed parts of her that made her shiver in delight. "Why does the water feel this way?" she asked, wide eyed and breathless.

"It's the bath oil. Feels good?"

A moan of complaint slipped free when Christa lifted her effortlessly out of the joyous delight of her first bath. She was dripping water everywhere before Christa stretched out her legs, then turned Wanda so she faced the window before lowering her between them. This time, water lapped over the edge, splashing the floor.

"We're making a mess," she protested, peering over the edge at the beautiful flooring, hating to spoil it.

Before her eyes, the water disappeared, and she glanced back at a mischievous, grinning demon who shrugged. "What's the point in being able to do these things, if I can't do them for us?"

How could Wanda disagree when she benefited from not having to get out of the bath to clean the mess?

Christa lay back, her hair gathered up and twirled in a band that appeared, held away from the water. This side of Christa, who looked a little less put together with tendrils of hair curling around her beautiful face, giving her an air of vulnerability, captivated Wanda. She rested her head on a small pillow and smiled invitingly at Wanda, patting her ample breasts. "Come lie back and immerse yourself in the wonders of a hot bath."

It wasn't funny how fast Wanda complied, already in love with how the hot, oily water felt gliding over her skin as she relaxed back. Christa ran her fingers through Wanda's curls and did what she had done to her own hair. Wanda's eyelashes fluttered, her whole body singing in pleasure as water lapped over her breasts, the bubbles tickling her nipples. "This is…"

"Amazing? Life changing?" Christa finished, sounding utterly smug and with every right.

Wanda was positive she would never look at her lake bath with quite the same enthusiasm. "Yes, it is. How will I ever want to go back to the lake to bathe again?"

Christa's giggles jiggled her breasts against Wanda's back. "My love, why would you need to when this is right on our tree step."

Wanda looked back and up at Christa, grinning widely. "Aren't we the lucky ones?"

"I'm bonded to you, of course that makes me the lucky one."

Blushing, Wanda settled back, looking out at her trees, sighing in complete contentment. "That makes six of us."

The tree branches swayed in agreement, and Christa's laughter increased. The girlish sound caused a rush of desire in Wanda's lower belly.

"It's a pity they'll never know the joys of having a bubble bath."

Wanda shut her eyes and ran her hands over her heavy breasts, the water seducing her with its silky texture.

"My love… what are you doing?" Christa murmured sexily, her breath touching Wanda's ear.

"Sharing with our girls," she moaned.

"Then let me help."

Chapter Twenty-Two

Christa

"Are you sure you don't need another bath? You got sweaty picking the peaches for Dougal." The hopefulness was hard to miss when she also gave Christa a pleading smile.

Wanda was an utter delight. Her introduction to bathing in hot water was a revelation. The rest of the house, and all the changes Christa had made, went unnoticed. Wanda had one fixation with the house, and it was the bathroom.

She usually bathed in the lake every morning, but that had stopped and now she wanted to bathe twice a day, even when she had done nothing to warrant it.

Christa struggled to keep her amusement to herself, especially when their trees actively encouraged Wanda to make as much use of the bathroom as possible. Most likely because she liked to share exactly how it made her feel to have the scented, oily water caressing her skin. Yes, she was an utter delight.

Whether it was the magic protection the king had given the forest, or the stone Wanda kept tucked into the bodice of whatever she wore, she was more confident. There was none of the fear she'd displayed before Asmodeus's visit. Something that Silas had remarked on, which made the trip to the demon realm worth the upset.

Wanda nudged her arm. "Do you?"

She bit the inside of her cheek to hold back her laughter. "I didn't get sweaty, my love. It was one small basket of peaches I took to leave for him."

There was something wrong with Dougal, Christa felt it through the trees. He visited infrequently now, and when he did, the trees behaved differently than before.

Wanda ran a hand down her arm. "You feel a little sticky to me."

The laughter escaped this time, and she lifted Wanda to kiss her soundly on the lips. "Do you want a bath, my love?"

Wanda didn't quite pull off the nonchalant shrug while not looking directly at Christa, blushing a rosy pink.

"I... maybe... okay, yes, I do," she muttered sheepishly, eyelashes dipping. "I've a lot of catching up to do, missing out for all those years." She rested her head on Christa's shoulder and sighed forlornly. "Why didn't Silas explain how wonderful a bath can be? He had one and never once mentioned it." She was miffed at her brother, that came across loudly.

"Isn't this a little like the burgers you told him were bad for you?" she pointed out, chuckling. Wanda got things stuck in her head and it took a lot to remove the belief.

The next sigh was heartfelt. "I suppose." She lifted her head, curls bouncing around her face. "But I know how good it is now, and it's more fun when we have a bath together."

Christa couldn't argue with that, especially as Wanda's sexy musk increased.

One thought and they were back in the bathroom, the bath filled and scented, this time with orange blossom. They had fun trying out the different bath oils and had gone through about a third of the collection so far. The orange blossom was Wanda's favorite up to now.

Christa placed her down, wanting to remove Wanda's dress herself. She got a heavy-lidded, dreamy expression whenever Christa took the time to strip her clothes from her body.

Her breasts rose and fell quickly as Christa knelt on a pillow she conjured, removing the big height difference between them. This put her at eye level with the beautiful breasts that were flushed with arousal as Christa peeled the dress down over Wanda's arms and pushed it over the soft swell of her hips, letting it pool at her bare feet.

Christa's gaze traveled over the soft, pale curves down to the lace and silk thong that revealed how excited Wanda was. The damp, white silk barely covered her mound. Wanda, who never wore underwear, had taken to wearing the lace and silk thongs that Christa had a thing for when she explained how much she loved how they looked on her. They teased Christa's desires when they covered Wanda's sex, the silk barely hiding the delights beneath. But they left her creamy skinned, ample bottom exposed to her roaming hands.

Her breathing hitched when Christa came closer, licking at the lace band over Wanda's rounded belly. "I know you want to get in the water, but you smell delicious, my love." Her eyes held Wanda's as she ran her tongue down the front of the silk, right between the folds of Wanda's sex, seeing her pupils dilate. The color bled to black. Her arousal was heady. Burying her nose in the silk, Christa inhaled deeply, tasting Wanda's musky flavor.

Wanda's legs wobbled and parted, giving Christa better access as hands landed on her shoulders, nails digging in as she mewled. Just the day before, Christa had waxed the hair from between Wanda's thighs. Her bare mound looked soft and inviting, even with the silk covering.

Another thing that had taken a little persuading, Christa had poured oil over her bare mound and got Wanda to run her fingers over it, explaining and projecting exactly how it felt. She didn't need to ask again, now Christa wanted to bury her face in between Wanda's legs and feel that silky skin against her mouth. Her tongue. Her face.

Breath chugging in and out with excitement, she sat back and hooked her fingers under the lace band, slowly tugging it down. Taking her time, she built the sexual tension between them.

Wanda's nipples were flushed, hard peaks. Her thighs shook as Christa revealed her pink, slick pussy. Her scent was intoxicating, and Christa felt the flood of her own desire pooling between her legs. She didn't rush while she peeled the panties ever so slowly to Wanda's ankles. "Lift up, my love."

Clutching tighter at her shoulders, Wanda whimpered, lifting her left foot. Slipping off the lace and silk, she pushed aside the dress. Repeating it with the other leg until she stood naked before her. Her pussy, no longer hidden by curls, revealed how flushed and swollen it was with arousal.

"Oh my love, look at how pretty your pussy looks."

Wanda groaned, and Christa witnessed her desire slicking her thighs, ramping up her need to see more. "Part your legs and hold your pussy lips open for me. Let me see how much you want my touch."

Dark pools of want stared down at Christa as Wanda did as asked with trembling fingers. It was pure excitement, and Christa felt it combine with her own desire. Their bond gave her a boost like she'd stuck her finger in an electrical socket. "Can you feel how wet you are?"

Wanda's desire glistened on her open sex and Christa gave in, moving forward, close enough to still hold Wanda's gaze. "Watch me," she murmured, using her demon's tongue to reach Wanda and hold position. Long enough,

Christa dragged it from back to front, tickling her asshole because although Wanda didn't ask for her to touch her there, she often pushed into Christa's touch when her fingers skimmed over her pink hole.

A whimpered moan came with a hip rock back, then forward, as if she couldn't decide where she wanted Christa to lick more. That was fine, because Christa was going to taste her wherever she wanted. Wetting her finger, she moved her hand behind Wanda, slipping it between her spread legs. Wanda gasped, her skin dewy and flushed at the next touch to her asshole. When Christa lapped between her spread lips, Wanda's desire easily coated her tongue, encouraging her to continue to twirl her finger over the quivering bud while lapping at her clit.

Swollen, it peeked past the hood and Christa sucked it into her mouth, flicking her tongue over the sensitive flesh. Teasing it, she circled her tongue over the throbbing flesh. Wanda's body shook as she became more vocal. The noises bounced off the tiles as Christa slid her tongue inside, thrusting slowly. She wiggled it while making noises so it vibrated, then withdrew to suck Wanda's desire into her mouth, only to repeat.

"Oh… oh… oh… there… oh… please… more…."

Her ass canted backwards, and Christa slid her finger further forward to push it into her soaking pussy then, using it to slick her between her ass cheeks, pushed the tip of her finger inside the tight rim as she sucked hard on Wanda's clit. Wanda cried out, a fresh flood of desire filling Christa's mouth. She groaned as Wanda's legs gave way, flopping forward, causing Christa to grab on to one hip. Her fingers sank into her soft flesh to steady her, while the noises, taste and her face buried in Wanda triggered Christa's orgasm.

She didn't stop licking and sucking Wanda, riding the feelings coming from Wanda as she creamed her own panties until they soaked her clothing. When they both stopped shuddering and their breathing slowed down, Wanda was no longer holding any of her own weight, so Christa translocated them into the bath.

Wanda groaned anew as the oily water ran over her sensitive sex. Her thighs parted, pushing Christa's against the wide tub. Christa ran her nose down the side of Wanda's neck, kissing softly against her beating pulse. "Stroke your pussy for me, tell me how it feels now it's bare and wet."

Wanda turned her head, pushing her hot cheek into Christa's neck, but her hand was moving.

"Lift your hips up, my love, I want to watch."

She moaned, her breath hitting Christa's damp skin in small bursts. Christa watched the fingers slide over and dip down between Wanda's thighs. With a thought, more oil poured over Wanda's hand. She bit her lip, the sounds muffled, her fingers moving. "Tell me how it feels."

"So… slick… I don't wanna stop touching," she finished on a gasp as Christa filled her thoughts with how much she loved that.

"You don't need to. We can do this all day," Christa murmured throatily. "All night. Whenever you want to."

Connected as they were, she felt Wanda crest on the next wave of arousal, coming harder, and still her fingers never stopped stroking. "That's it, my love, do what feels good."

Wanda mouthed at her throat, then her teeth nipped at her flesh and Christa shook when the feeling pulsed directly in her sex. Then Wanda bit harder, marking her.

Christa got sideswiped by her own release. She shook hard enough to have water slipping over the floor unobserved, both women lost in the joint pleasure. Christa's demon cries of pleasure filled her mind as Wanda lapped up her blood, groaning and writhing as she came again.

Gasping, and struggling to stop sinking under the water, Christa had a 'come to the demoness' goddess' moment.

Holy fuck, what was that?

Chapter Twenty-Three

Wanda

She wasn't sure what woke her, but Wanda lay listening to Christa's soft breathing. She could tell from the rhythm that her love was deeply asleep. The leaves rustled in the gentle breeze, but no other sound carried in her nook.

When she shut her eyes, she found herself unable to settle. Something wasn't quite right beyond her trees. She carefully untangled herself from Christa where they had fallen asleep after their epic…

Her body heated, desire building fast in her core. It was shocking how, even without really thinking too hard about what they had done the day before, the arousal continued to hum in her sex. They had spent hours re-topping the bath with hot water while Wanda had touched herself multiple times, bringing herself to orgasm. Insatiable, one orgasm after another, the silky feel of her bare mound doing something indescribable to her, which only became enhanced further with Christa whispering her naughty commands in her ear.

What shocked her was that she had bitten Christa. She buried her head in her hands, hiding her embarrassment at the lack of remorse she felt at such an action. Such a show of possessiveness. She wanted to claim that the mark on Christa's throat made her feel bad, but the taste of Christa's blood had ignited her own.

A sound beyond the trees drew her attention, and she reached for the stone the king had given her on pure instinct. It pulsed against her skin, and she identified what had woken her.

Is the king outside? she asked her girls, choosing not to wake Christa yet.

He is.

What is he doing?

He's just standing, staring at nothing, in the orchard.

Is he injured? A feeling of concern came, despite a niggle of worry about approaching the king alone.

No, he is unharmed, but his emotions are strong. Unbalanced.

Doing her best not to overthink what she was about to do, she crept out of her trees. *Close back up to shield Christa.*

They did as she requested, and a moment later, dressed, she walked silently towards the king, who looked like a statue in the moonlight, standing in her orchard.

When he didn't seem to notice her, she asked softly, "Is there a reason you're standing there like a statue in the moonlight?"

He glanced at her, his eyes pools of black in the moonlight.

When all he did was stare for longer than was polite, she checked her dress was covering everything. Her hair swayed over her shoulders as she used the moonlight to guide her closer to him.

His distress tainted the air, and she felt the weight of his immense sadness. "My trees are nervous even when I know you mean us no harm." The stone that sat inside her trees was proof of that.

"We do not," he rasped, clearly struggling to hold on to what was causing his pain.

It was easy to recall how the fear had not returned after his visit, even now, as he stood silently watching her. She had a lot to be grateful to this demon for. If she could help, she would.

"Then did you get lost in the forest searching for Dakata?" she persisted, attempting to find a way to get him to talk about what was on his mind.

The breeze picked up and her dress fluttered about her legs, drawing her attention to what she hadn't initially noticed—though how she missed the nudity of an over seven-foot demon was beyond her. Her head quirked to the side, keeping her gaze from dipping. His emotions had been her immediate concern, not the lack of clothing.

Searching for something to say, she waffled, "Although the lateness of the hour would suggest that calling now may not be appropriate."

She nearly sighed in relief when, a moment later, he wore a long, flowing robe and tied it at his waist.

"Where is Christa?" he asked, yet she sensed that was not what he wanted to say.

"She has some business to take care of in the demon realm, she will be along shortly. Did you wish to speak to her?" The lie rolled off her tongue, because going to get Christa was not what she thought the king wanted, she just couldn't say why.

"I… there… yes… see…" he stuttered, not looking at her but at the ground.

Wanda was more attuned to the forest than many understood. Wanda felt Dougal's distress, the building emotions he struggled to contain until she felt him release them. They shook her trees, giving her a blast of what had upset him. Dougal kept his personal life to himself, and Wanda honored that. She did, however, know there was something between him and this demon. The king's presence in the forest, when he came to meet her, had not been the first time.

The king's essence was there in the earth, the roots of the trees, the plants. For that to happen, he must have visited many times and had a connection to the one being who nurtured the forest since its inception—Dougal. She would never speak of it to anyone, it was not her place, but here and now she felt compelled to continue to talk, to see if it helped the demon. "Is it about Dougal?"

The quiet question got his eyes narrowing on her, but she never flinched. "What do you know? What has he said?"

She giggled before she could stop it at how his eyes actually glowed with hope. He was that easy to read. "You and he are a lot alike. Dougal has said nothing to me." Her expression lost the playfulness and turned serious. "I am part of these trees, therefore part of the roots that reach into the ground. There is little in the forest that escapes the true forest dwellers, and I would say all that Dougal has been feeling of late, we feel, too." She gave him what she felt he needed—the truth.

"Feel? What does he feel?" he asked, the words tumbling from his lips.

That was easy to answer. "Everything."

He huffed, and she sensed his ire in the change in the breeze against her bare arms. "What kind of answer is that?"

"The only one." She came closer, her need to touch him when she understood his fear better than most driving her to reach out and place a hand on his arm. "Fear can kill everything that is good with its shadow. It will smother a heart, the love within it, if one lets it."

Asmodeus stared down at her hand as if not quite believing she had the audacity to touch him.

The sob that tore from his throat was harrowing and made her heart ache for him. The next one brought him to the ground, he sat like his legs could no longer support him and Wanda followed, sitting next to him, patting his hand gently. "That's it. Let it out."

As he shook, sobbing uncontrollably, she entwined her fingers as best she could in the massive, clawed hand, feeling him clinging to her. "It's a heavy burden you carry. Put it down a while, then you might see your way more clearly."

She knew the moment Christa woke and felt her panic at finding her gone. She blocked her, knowing any request she would deny.

Tell her I'm fine, you must keep her inside for now.

She is concerned.

I'm fine, she will know this. King Asmodeus is of no threat to us. He would be upset to be caught like this by one of his own kind.

She sat in silence, listening to his sobs quieten, while never letting go of her hand. When he finally looked up, her bottom was numb. His tear swollen, misery filled eyes met hers and she could feel his unease surface.

"This is a private moment. Just between us."

He gave a jerky nod after a brief hesitation. "Thank you for your patience with me." It was the first time she'd heard him be humble.

"You gave me a gift, took my fear away. I would say that spending time with *a friend*, sitting in the moonlight, is not a chore if I gave you a little of the solace you gave me."

"You are a wise woman."

She shook her head, curls tickling over her neck as they moved. "If I had been as wise as you say, I would not have rejected my blissful one in the beginning."

He sighed heavily. "Then that makes two of us."

Still holding his hand, she squeezed it. "The thing with a blissful one is that it's never too late to change what is into what should be. A wise troll taught me that, just saying."

Even in the moonlight, she could see the way his shoulders went from stooped to straight. It appeared he'd come to a decision.

She hoped it would give both him and Dougal what they wanted. "Maybe you should go back to your realm and get some sleep before you decide about your… future."

He rose stiffly, rubbing at his backside, before offering Wanda.a hand to help her up. "Please, all I ask is that you don't speak of my visit… for now."

"Of course." She tugged the huge hand, getting a wide-eyed, startled look before he went with her tugging and bent closer to her. Not overthinking it, she gave him an awkward hug because he was just too big to wrap her arms around.

"We're friends. I don't suspect you have many of those in your position. I'm here whenever you wish to talk." She pulled back, dropping her arms, and offered a soft smile. "Day or night."

"You are more than I deserve." He bowed and, in a blink, was gone.

Seconds later, Christa burst out of the trees behind her. Wild hair flowed behind her as she rushed to her, naked in her demon form, patting her down as if to check she was unharmed.

Wanda giggled, getting swept off the forest floor. Kisses were peppered all over her face as Christa murmured, "I was so worried. Why was the king here? Why did you block me? Tell the girls not to let me outside? Do you know how stressful this was?"

The questions kept coming, and Christa didn't take a breath to pause and let her answer. Wanda took matters into her own hands and slipped her arms around Christa's neck and kissed her.

Her lips parted invitingly, feeling Christa's pounding heart beating hard against hers. "I'm fine. All is well. He just needed a quiet place to think," she whispered between kisses. "Now, let's go back to bed, where you can reassure both your demon and human side that I'm perfectly un-harmed."

Christa's dark eyes glowed in the moonlight. "That could take the rest of the night."

She gave what she hoped was a seductive smile. "Maybe the girls need to help?"

"I love how you think."

So do we.

They all laughed as the branches lifted them both into the nook and closed the world out.

Chapter Twenty-Four

Christa

Wanda had left the nook before Christa and was outside checking over her trees and the surrounding plants, something the girls explained she had stopped doing after the kidnapping. They were clacking branches, showing how happy they were for Wanda to be acting more like how she was before the attack.

Christa didn't dwell on what couldn't be changed, just focused on the happiness she felt through her bond from

Wanda. Coming out of the nook, dressed in a vest top and shorts, she walked barefoot to the little area where Dougal liked to set up his fire pit. It gave Christa the best view of the whole orchard, and her blissful one.

A pillow appeared on the log as she went to sit. She had no issue living in a tree, but saw no reason not to have some of the other creature comforts she enjoyed. Like a little padding for her ample bottom, because no one liked to sit on hard surfaces when they didn't need to. The morning sun was high enough in the sky to make the dew-drops on the leaves and blades of grass glisten in its light. Tiny rainbows inside each drop gave beauty despite their size, as did the tiny dryad wandering through the orchard, touching, stroking and encouraging the life around her to grow. Having not witnessed it before, Christa quickly became mesmerized at witnessing how a simple touch gave life to wilted flowers or leaves curling at the edges. How every plant swayed towards Wanda in greeting as she approached, looking as though she floated above the grassy ground.

The energy in the orchard increased. A delicate balance of nature working with Wanda's gift. The green of her eyes deepened to that of the forest. Sun haloed her curls, which swished gently around her shoulders, and laughter tin-kling at a playing flower tickling her wrist when she went to move on carried on the breeze.

Joy. She radiated it. Pure and simple joy.

Christa had, on some level, understood the way Wanda liked to live, yet witnessing her now in her true element, using her gift, struck how fundamental she was to the life of the plants, trees, and shrubs. She rested her elbows on her knees, cupping her chin, and followed Wanda's progress, thoughts of getting breakfast for them both forgotten at the delight in front of her.

This was what the demons had stolen from her.

Don't be sad. Look at her.

She could do nothing but look at the wonder of nature. The fears she'd kept firmly locked down after finding Wanda alone with the king had no place inside her. Whatever had happened the night before with Asmodeus and Wanda, her blissful one was not letting on. No, her questions had gone unanswered with a cryptic smile. They had been outside for hours and, with the trees stopping her from leaving the nook, she could only imagine the worst. Yet Wanda had been... relaxed, playful after. Now this.

Christa, who had cursed the king last night, this morning, sent up a gift of thanks for somehow releasing Wanda fully from the chains that held her hostage within herself and her trees.

"Why are you staring at me like that?" Wanda called from the other side of the orchard, not stopping what she was doing.

Her lips tugging into a smile, Christa called back, "And how is that, my love?"

Wanda met her gaze, eyes crinkling at the edges as a wide grin spread like the sunshine appearing from behind a cloud. Bright and bold, it warmed Christa to her very core. "Like it's the first time you've seen me."

Christa rose, eyed her bare feet, and conjured a pair of sneakers. She wasn't at the stage of thinking pebbles and twigs were comfortable to walk on. Avoiding them was harder to do when she seldom looked down at where she was walking when she had Wanda to stare at. "It feels like it."

Wanda waited where she was, her dress skimming the ground and over her bare toes. "And why is that?" she questioned when Christa reached her.

"You look… *free*."

The smile grew brighter, if at all possible, as she hooked an arm through Christa's and walked towards the nearest peach tree. "I feel free, although that doesn't quite capture the sense inside me."

Christa brushed a stray curl from Wanda's cheek when they stopped at the tree laden with peaches. "Do you need to find a word to encapsulate the feeling?"

"No. No, I don't." She reached up, and the branches lowered to stop her stretching. "I believe Dougal would enjoy some peaches today." Wanda gave her a look of expectation. "A basket would be good?"

A moment later, Christa held one out to Wanda, who took it. "Thank you."

Christa plucked several peaches from the branches and placed them in the basket Wanda held, considering how to broach what was on her mind. With how Wanda was, it made what she was about to suggest easier—she hoped—when it meant introducing Wanda to her family.

Dakata had nudged her demon, and she admitted to blocking the family because of how things were with Wanda. And yes, she'd gone beyond the nook to the house, but that was for a purpose, the bathroom. Christa shut down her train of thought when it was keen to head to the time spent there. It would derail what she wanted to talk about. She very much desired for her brothers to meet the most important person in her life. She'd never felt compelled to introduce girlfriends she had briefly dated before. This was different and regardless of how annoying her brothers could be with her as the only female, they loved her and she them.

"What is on your mind?"

Christa, about to place a peach in the nearly full basket, looked at Wanda. The only sign of concern was the wrinkle at the bridge of her nose. "My family."

"You miss them?"

Wanda, like Christa, blocked her thoughts on the subject, so it was harder to get a read from her. "I do. I wonder if maybe it would be nice to invite them to dinner, or lunch, at the house. I could cook."

"You cook?"

Wanda's wide eyes made Christa laugh. "I love to cook. It can be very relaxing, putting on a playlist and making food that feeds the soul."

Intrigue came through their bond. "What foods feed the soul?"

"A thick vegetable soup with homemade crusty bread. A chocolate fudge cake. Creamy sauces rich with wine and fish…" Christa's belly rumbled as she continued to recite everything she loved to cook for herself and enjoyed eating.

Wanda wiped her lips, almost as if she was drooling. "You're making me hungry, though I've never tried any of the things you mention. A creamy fish sauce, what is that like?"

Christa had to stop herself from asking what planet Wanda had been on, knowing that would be utterly ridiculous. Wanda had little contact with the outside world and freely admitted a burger was an adventure.

"You have never tried fish?" she clarified, just to be sure.

Wanda's curls bounced as she shook her head. "Is it as tasty as a burger?"

The eagerness was hard to resist. "More so, and actually healthier."

She gave Christa a bashful grin. "Could you make a meal with fish for me so I can try?"

"Of course. Shall I organize to have that for lunch with my family?" she persisted, going back to the original conversation.

There was no hesitation that Christa noticed when Wanda nodded. "Will you make it yourself? Can I watch?"

"Of course, and yes. You can be my kitchen assistant." Christa liked the idea a lot.

"What does that entail?"

Christa took the basket of peaches from Wanda and, with a thought, she sent the basket to where Dougal spent most of his time in the forest. "Come on, I'll give you a preview. I think I should introduce you to hot chocolate fudge cake. Cake for breakfast is most definitely a must."

Christa struggled to keep from laughing aloud at Wanda's serious expression as she eyed Christa's bowl and then her own. "I think I've missed a step."

Wanda had wanted to learn how to make a cake when Christa had set up the ingredients on the counter, so she'd conjured more unable to deny her anything, even when it turned out Wanda was completely inept in the kitchen.

The apron Christa had tied around Wanda's waist to pro-tect her dress was a war-zone of stains that she had smeared on the white fabric. They weren't just on the apron. No, Wanda had smears of flour, what might be egg, and chocolate over one side of her face, leading from her chin down her neck somehow. There was flour and melted chocolate coating her curls from the amount of times Wanda forgot and used her gooey covered hands to push back her hair to better see what Christa was doing to follow the instructions.

The once pristine kitchen was an utter mess. Somehow Wanda had covered every surface in some sticky, floury or gooey substance. Some of which Christa actually couldn't identify an hour into the lesson.

"No, it's fine, we need to transfer the mix into the greased tins."

"Are you sure mine looks right?" Wanda looked once more from her bowl to Christa's, frowning. "Why is mine a different color to yours?" She jabbed at the mix with the wooden spoon as if that would solve the issue. "Mine is definitely paler than yours."

Christa snort-giggled, doing her very best to hold back her amusement with how sulky Wanda sounded. "It's probably just not got as much chocolate in as mine."

The frown deepened, and Wanda's eyes narrowed. "I used the same amount as you."

Christa bit her lip, hard, at seeing exactly where all the chocolate had gone that was not in Wanda's bowl. She coughed. "It's fine, my love. It will look exactly like mine when it's baked."

Wanda didn't look convinced, and rightly so, but Christa didn't have the heart to point out why. "So, use the stick of butter I cut in half and rub it around the baking tin. We have to make sure to cover the bottom and up the sides so the mixture doesn't glue itself to the tin when it cooks."

Wanda followed her instructions, butter covering not only the inside but the outside, too. Christa noticed Wanda liked to be very heavy-handed—with every-thing.

Christa went back to biting her lip when she offered to help and got her hand slapped away. "I can do it."

Ten minutes later, Wanda pushed her tin into the heat-ed oven, grinning. "How long do we have to wait?"

"Forty minutes. But we need to make the chocolate ganache next, for the center and the topping."

Wanda's brows arched up as she looked at the emp-ty pile of packets sat on the table. "I haven't got any chocolate left."

Christa gave her a reassuring smile, conjuring more. What they'd already used was enough to give all the children of a small country cavities. She pointed at the counter. "We've got plenty."

A look of relief followed as Wanda went over and picked up the three giant sized packets, clutching them in her buttery hands. "Where are your packets?"

It was too much, and Christa howled with laughter, going over to Wanda and hugging her, regardless of the mess she was in. All Christa could smell was chocolate as she nuzzled her curls. "I love you."

Her neck arched back to look up at Christa with uncertainty. "I love you too, but why are you laughing?"

She didn't resist and bent to give the messy cheek a lick, scooping off some of the chocolate. "Because I forgot how much fun it was to bake."

"Oh…" The uncertainty disappeared, Wanda's eyes sparkling with excitement. "What else shall we make after this?"

Christa kissed the tip of her floury nose. "Whatever you want."

Chapter Twenty-Five

Wanda

Despite how wonderful the house smelled, Wanda's nerves were getting the better of her. She had assisted Christa in the kitchen, while she made all the wonderful things for their lunch. That said, given the knots forming in her belly, she wasn't sure she was going to be able to eat a single bite of the tempting foods. Wanda had discovered she had been missing out on a lot.

Until Silas had gone into the city and realized the delights of cheeseburgers, Wanda had tasted nothing but fruits, plants, herbs and vegetables. Most in their very basic form. She had not felt inclined to try doing much with them.

The meat patties were delicious and temptingly good, so whenever Silas had gone to town, she had wanted one. And yes, since Christa had introduced her to pizza, she enjoyed it, too. Not as much as the burgers, though. They had been her favorite *until* she'd tried the chocolate fudge cake. It was a revelation. Not hers particularly, though she couldn't say why, except it wasn't as moist and light as Christa's.

Cake was a party in the mouth, full of wonderful flavor and sweetness. So much so, Wanda had gorged herself to the point of feeling queasy, even when Christa had warned her it was very rich, and Wanda wasn't used to eating it.

Yes, chocolate fudge cake most certainly beat having a burger any day of any week, which was why Wanda found herself encouraging Christa back up to the house and into the kitchen, *not the bathroom*. Although they still spent a lot of time in the bathroom, to clean up Wanda, who couldn't appear to keep everything in the bowl, the same as Christa.

It was a mystery.

"Stop chewing on your lip, you'll make it bleed." Christa slipped an arm around the front of her as she drew her back against her warm, scented body. Their size difference made her feel delicate when she hugged her this way.

She released her lip, tracing it with the tip of her tongue to feel the marks her teeth had left behind. "Do you think they'll like me?"

"They'll love you."

She turned in Christa's arms, stretching her neck to look at her. "Liking is fine. I only need your love."

"You say the sweetest things." Christa kissed the center of her forehead.

"Knock knock. Is it safe to come in? Do I need to avert my eyes? I could hear some pretty mushy talk going on."

Christa rolled her eyes, turning her attention to the doorway the voice was coming from. "Behave Luka and get your backside in here."

A man dressed in a smart gray suit and a black shirt walked into the kitchen and Wanda could see the likeness to Dakata. Though he was as tall, he wasn't as bulky across the chest as Dakata. Behind him came another man, also dressed in a suit, but it was navy paired with a pale blue shirt. Neither man wore a tie, their top buttons undone. He was slimmer, and his smile was more like Christa's.

"Benra, it's nice to see you arrived on time."

Jet black brows rose, and sapphire blue eyes twinkled with cheekiness. "I wanted to see what got our sister moving to the sticks and hiding out in a tree, no less." He glanced about the kitchen. "Though, this doesn't look like tree living to me. Did you move all your stuff from the house in the city?"

"I did and shut up, you are giving my blissful one a poor impression." Christa grinned at Wanda. "This is Benra and Luka." Her attention returned to her brothers. "Be nice, I told her you were all loveable."

Benra laughed at her rebuke. "I don't think that's possible when she's bonded with you. And of course we are loveable, I mean,"—his hand waved down his body—"look at me."

Christa let go of Wanda, shaking her head. "You never change." She went to Benra and grabbed his cheeks, giving him a sisterly peck on the lips. "And if you don't behave, you won't get any of my special chocolate cheesecake."

He clutched at his chest, faking a look of distress as Luka watched on, chuckling. "Not that!"

"I can see it's going to be business as usual," Dakata muttered, coming in with Silas at his side.

"There's sweet cheeks." Benra went to Silas, and Dakata punched his brother's arm when he went to touch Silas. "Ouch," he hissed, rubbing at his arm.

"Keep your damn hands to yourself. He's my blissful one, find your own!"

Wanda stared in amazement as they continued to argue and smack at each other. She looked at Silas to see if he was as confused as her by the way they were. He gave them all an indulgent look and shrugged at Wanda.

"Lunch will get cold if you all continue to bicker like children."

Christa had bickered right along with them, but Wanda decided not to point that out.

By the time they were all sitting at the table, it became a competition about who could speak loud enough to be heard over the others. Wanda's temples throbbed a little, and her worry about eating ceased when she spent most of her time staring wide eyed at the brothers and Christa. It was most entertaining to watch them when they were all so happy to be together. Happiness filled the dining area.

Silas, like her, didn't get to say much, but he tucked into the food, groaning in approval as he tried all the dishes covering the table.

"The food is delicious, Christa," Silas murmured minutes later when there was a break in the conversation.

"I helped," Wanda said, though she could admit she'd probably been more of a hindrance.

"You did indeed, my love." Christa's smile gave Wanda a warm feeling in the center of her chest, even when all the men looked at her.

"She's real bossy," Benra said in a stage whisper. "You have to learn to distract her."

Wanda giggled, feeling included in a way she hadn't considered was possible. "I already know how to distract her, don't worry."

Everyone burst out laughing when Christa blushed bright pink. "That you do." She nudged Wanda's full plate of food closer to her. "Now eat up, or you won't get dessert."

Wanda searched Christa's expression. Wanda couldn't quite tell if she was serious and having licked the spoon clean earlier, she spiked a crispy potato on the end of her fork. She dipped it in the peppercorn sauce and popped it into her mouth, and waved her empty fork at Christa. No one wanted to miss out on dessert, especially when it was a chocolate and cream combo.

This got more laughter from the others.

She mumbled around the potato, "I licked the spoon, I'm not daft."

Christa placed a hand on her knee, squeezing gently, and answered Luka's question. The sense of connection was there. The life of a dryad was a lonely existence until they found their tree. There were so few of them left in the world, and they preferred their own company to that of other dryads. Her parents were the same. They had no time for her or Silas.

When Silas left, Wanda had felt cast adrift and quickly followed her brother because she much preferred company to being alone.

As her eyes swept around the table, the four siblings were the epitome of family. Her own weren't the ones to give her a sense of what an actual family was like. No, that had been Silas and Dougal.

Dougal. Her heart ached at what her conversation with the king had revealed. What he must have suffered, both of them. Yet, she'd felt the burst of life, of energy in the forest and understood Asmodeus had finally chosen what he wanted over his fear.

"So Wanda, is it you I have to thank for being left to do all the work?"

Wanda's gaze flew to Luka, the piece of meat she was in the process of swallowing caught in her throat. Coughing violently, Christa smacked her on the back, reaching for her water glass. "Here, have a drink." She glared at Luka. "Did you have to say that!"

"Sorry."

"So you should be," Christa snapped back, holding the glass to Wanda's lips despite the fact she'd reached out to take it herself.

"It's me you should blame," Silas said, chuckling. "It is Dakata's business."

"He has a choice. I could get someone else to run the business," Dakata replied, jabbing his fork at Luka, his gaze searching Silas's, who smiled guilelessly.

"You love it." Benra stared Luka down. "I've never seen you so happy, so give it up pretending to be annoyed."

Luka gave him a big ass grin and shoving a honey roasted carrot in his mouth.

"I'm fine." Wanda gently nudged the glass away when Christa tried to drown her.

"It's a good job, or someone would have gotten their demon ass kicked," she threatened Luka, who just laughed at her.

"Children," Dakata groaned, but his eyes held a wealth of amusement.

It never stopped. They continued on through the meal, onto dessert and clean up. They all helped, notwithstanding the moaning and complaining. By the time everyone was getting ready to leave, the sun had dipped in the sky and Wanda found herself with three additional brothers.

"Don't leave it so long next time," Benra murmured, kissing Christa's cheek, before moving to do the same to Wanda.

"Not if Christa is cooking," Luka replied, holding up the covered dish of leftovers.

More cheek kisses and finally they were gone, leaving Wanda mentally exhausted, but content.

Christa sat down on the couch and dragged Wanda down next to her. She groaned and laid her head back on the couch, closing her eyes. "Remind me again why I thought this would be a good idea? They always give me a damn headache."

"They are loud." Wanda agreed with that. She rested her head on Christa's shoulder, looking out the window. The dipping sun silhouetted her trees. They swayed in the breeze and encouraged her home. "It's time to go home," she murmured.

Christa moved, dislodging her head to look at her. A softness to her gaze came when she glanced at the orchard. "Yes, it is. They missed us."

In that moment, Wanda was truly happy they had the house to use for Christa and Wanda's family, but that their home in the trees would always be just for them.

She kissed Christa's throat, trailing open-mouthed kisses down the column of her neck, reaching the exposed collarbone which she traced with her tongue. "Take us there."

"As you wish, my love."

In the blink of an eye, Wanda lay naked on a lush bed of leaves with Christa lying at her side. Her hand stroked down her soft curves as the branches formed a nook around them, the overhead ones opening the canopy to allow them to watch the evening light fade and the soft evening air to caress Wanda's warm skin. She moaned as Christa came closer and kissed her, the taste of chocolate lingering on her tongue.

A languid feeling followed as Christa stroked over her heating flesh, murmuring words of love. "You are my world." Another kiss. "My everything." Another kiss. "My love," she groaned as Wanda went pliant.

"As you are mine," she answered breathlessly, losing herself in the world of love that her girls created, and Christa completed.

The End….

Well, it is for these pair. I hope you have loved this book as much as I have enjoyed dipping my toes and fingers into F/F romance. If you are interested in reading Dakata's and Merihem's stories, you'll find them on Amazon and any other retailers you use.

Warning: There is an epilogue to this story, but if you hate spoilers and want to finish this series, which is MM, then DO NOT READ ON. Secretary's Obsession is out on the 4th of March and the finale to the series is the King's Obsession out May 4th 2025, if you can wait that long to read the epilogue.

Steps away with an evil laugh.

Epilogue

Wanda

Eighteen Months Later

Wanda watched Christa while up to her elbows in flour. She was making a birthday cake for Dakata, and all that Wanda had done was get in the way. She couldn't help it, Christa was sexy when she got all creative in the kitchen.

"You are distracting me," Christa said in exasperation, making Wanda giggle because it was the truth.

"I thought I was helping?" She leaned closer to lick of the gooey cake mix from the spoon Christa pointed at her.

"That's it, go on, troublemaker." The love in her gaze took the sting away when Christa nudged her towards the door. "Go play in the orchard."

"If you're sure that's what you want?"

Christa released a deep belly laugh, shaking her head as she stepped back. "I've created a monster."

"One you love," Wanda held up her hands, backing towards the door, sensing Asmodeus heading towards her orchard. "But I'll go, just don't wash those spoons." She took the nudging Christa was doing to get her out of the kitchen in good spirit and left her to finish up without complaint.

Walking out into the sunshine, Wanda took a moment to breathe and acknowledge how wonderful her life was. To send out her gratitude to the universe for blessing her. They spent more time at the house than she'd ever have considered she'd like a year ago. In fact, it tended to be her that suggested they go there because it was a place where they explored Wanda's naivety of worldly things. Something that Christa loved to do that made life very fascinating and the house full of interesting drawers full of all kinds of gadgets and toys, both upstairs and down.

A smile spread at the sight of a dark head bobbing through the trees, holding a little bundle of joy. He'd brought Elara.

She picked up her pace. Her trees, feeling her excitement, swayed and lowered branches so that when Asmodeus reached them, Elara could grab at the peaches the child loved.

"There you are," Asmodeus said, while his daughter babbled baby speak.

"Christa is baking a cake for Dakata for his birthday and as I'm more of a hindrance than a help, she gave me a little nudge out the door, happy to see me leave."

"I'm sure she wasn't."

Wanda laughed at that. "You haven't seen how messy I get." Wanda looked at the little adorable troll-demon. "You know, don't you sweetheart, how messy Auntie Wanda gets?"

"Chocho... chocho."

Heat seared her cheeks at the babbles that sounded decidedly like chocolate. Wanda scooped the little girl who had just outed her on what she liked to treat her with and sat down on the log, avoiding the arched look that Asmodeus was aiming at her.

"So what adventures are you and Daddy going on today?" Wanda placed the little girl, who was holding onto a peach and waving it at her, in her lap.

Elara babbled at her, occasionally saying a word that made sense. She tried hard not to think about why the child always associated the word *chocho* with her. She didn't want her daddies not allowing her to come to the house to play with her. Wanda continued to practice cooking and baking, and she still had a few fails, but now they came with wins too, which she blended and fed to Elara when she was of an age to try.

Wanda had gotten Christa to do research on her cell phone about babies because neither of them had any experience and the last thing Wanda wanted to do was harm a child through lack of knowledge. Especially when Wanda and her love of all things chocolate had grown with each new kitchen experience with Christa. Who knew there were so many recipes you could use chocolate in? And she'd really wanted to share that delight with Elara when Wanda considered all the years she'd missed out on.

Asmodeus sat on the log, staring at them. Today he had dressed informally. He had become a frequent visitor to the orchard and often came to visit Wanda in the afternoons when he wasn't in his own realm. "Would you like to be a mother?"

Wanda blinked rapidly at the unexpected question. "I... erm... why do you ask?" she finished, flustered. Had she given having babies any thought? Yes, as had Christa after visits from Peni, Scott, and their children.

Christa's abilities did not fall into the realms of impregnating Wanda. The idea of traveling into the city to meet with medical people to do something in a laboratory was not something Wanda wanted, so it was pointless to wish for something that wasn't possible.

Wanda accepted this was her life, and she was truly happy with it.

He delicately brushed his large hand over the tiny head of his daughter, keeping his attention focused on Wanda. "You are wonderful with Elara."

Blushing at the compliment, something he rarely gave out, she inclined her head. "She's beautiful and easy to love, is she not?"

"She is."

As if the little girl knew her daddy was talking about her, she held out her arms and dropped the peach to reach for him. "Da-Da."

The look that appeared was one of complete adoration as he plucked her up and made several baby noises, then blew raspberries on her belly, making her giggle. Wanda bet few saw the powerful king as he was now and she felt honored to be gifted with the sight.

Elara's tiny hands grabbed out for his horns, and he let her reach them. His eyes glowed when she touched the silver tips. "That's daddy's girl, feel his power."

Father and daughter, a large red demon and a tiny pinky-gray one, stared at each other with an intensity that belied the child's age. She chattered nonsense, but Asmodeus gave her his full attention. "That's right, you will be queen one day and rule both realms."

Wanda was not surprised. Dougal's troll held immense power in this realm, as did Asmodeus in his. Together, the child they created would be a force to be reckoned with.

"You never answered my question."

"What... oh, I don't think about it because Christa and I have no way to conceive a child unless done medically, which neither of us wants. We don't want anyone touching the other." They were as possessive of each other and ideas of others touching intimately, neither would tolerate. Their feelings had grown and became as rooted as the trees in each other. No one got to touch Christa but Wanda and her girls.

"There are other ways."

Wanda glanced from Elara, who now lay in her father's arms, her eyelids drooping, as he gently rocked her. "What do you mean?"

"I mean, I have the power to help you or Christa conceive like I did for Peni and Merihem."

A squeak escaped as she gasped at the thought of Asmodeus impregnating her.

Why had Merihem let the king do that? Merihem and Peni brought their daughter to the forest to visit Silas and Dakata. She was a fluffy demon and as cute as Elara and as Wanda searched her memory, she saw no resemblance to the demon sat next to her. The girl was a mix of both her daddies.

"How... how did you do that?" Regardless of the blissful bond she shared with Christa, she would not have sex with a male demon. Hell no. And she knew Christa wouldn't, either.

He chuckled, rocking his daughter. "You need not fear, I do not need to touch you in that way. And I also like my balls intact, Dougal would not tolerate such nonsense."

She came a little closer, a flare of hope coming to life inside her. "Then how does it work?"

He brought a large hand close to hover over her belly, his eyes darkened until Wanda could see herself reflected in them. "Magic and hope."

His breath touched her face, and warmth spread through her. "What are you doing?"

"Giving your hope the magic," he murmured. "And the chance for you and Christa to decide."

He left not long later and Wanda couldn't have said what they'd talked about because all she could think about was what he'd said. He'd also given her a tiny black stone, which she had tucked into her pocket with the blood-red one.

"If I don't see another dirty dish for a year, it will be too soon," Christa moaned as she plonked herself down next to Wanda on their log, offering her a plate with a slice of decadently iced raspberry and white chocolate cake that smelled heavenly. "This is to make up for missing the spoon licking."

Wanda took the offering and the tiny cake fork, glancing at Christa, who looked disheveled. "You know you don't have to actually wash the dishes."

She shrugged and gave her a sheepish smile. "It's all part of it." She glanced about, her nose wrinkling. "Did Asmodeus pay you a visit?"

"He did…"

Her brows arched. "What is it? I got a blast of… actually, I'm not sure what I felt."

Wanda placed the plate down and turned to Christa, who frowned at the plate on the ground. Wanda took hold of Christa's hands, drawing her attention back to her. "He asked if I wanted to be a mom."

Pain came from Christa. "No, you don't get to carry blame for something we have no control over. Two girls don't get to have babies unless a medical person helps. We've talked about this."

"I would give you anything."

"My beloved, I know." Wanda held Christa's shimmering eyes, letting go of one hand to pull out the stone. She fed Christa all the love in her heart until a tear slid down her cheek. "What he's offering us is magic and hope, all we need to do is choose."

Christa came closer, her mouth claiming Wanda's in a heated kiss. "I choose you. Whatever else the universe has in store for us is just the icing on the cake."

It was all the answer Wanda needed, because Christa was right, the rest was just icing.

About the Author

E ccentric cake lover who has a passion for words of all kinds. I'm Jayne or JP, I live in the Isle of Man. A tiny place in the Irish sea where all the magic happens. I'm a confessed bookaholic and if I'm not writing I love to snuggle with a book or two…if you catch my drift.

If you're interested in keeping up to date, then I've a few places you can do that, and they're listed below. My website is where you'll find all the different Me's there are, LOL. As I travel this path into the future, I'm going to be writing in different genres so to stop there being any confusion I'll be writing under different pen names.

If you would like to give me any feedback or just have any questions, go ahead and friend me on Facebook, and I would be happy to answer anything. I hope you enjoyed this book and if you would also like to leave a review, then I would love to read your thoughts. Even if you just want to rate it, I'll be grateful

Thank you for being a part of my dream.

Goodreads

Tumblr

Bookbub

Instagram

Facebook

Facebook Author
page

JP Manx Minx's

More Books by the Author

S*tandalone*

When Fake Changed Everything

Christmas beyond Christmas

The Elves and the Bondage Daddy)

Agrippa My Heart

His Boy to Tease

Headshot

A Brat For Kinkmas

Hanging With Daddy

A Little Christmas Matty Secret

A Little Christmas Terrence

Music & Dreams

A Sucker For Christmas

Sweet Haven

Cruising Right Into Love

A Little Christmas Ollie

Series

Assassins To Order With Lisa Oliver

Marvin – Marvin and Ajani **in Audio**

Ben – Ben, Teilo & Nico **in Audio**

Duron – Duron & Beaumont **in Audio**

Conrad – Conrad & Kylo **in Audio**

Dancing With the Devil – Wyatt & James

Tangled Tentacles Series with Lisa Oliver

Alexi #1in audio

Victor #2 in audio

Todd #3 in audio

Markov # 4in audio

Kelvin # 5 in audio

Obsessions Series with Lisa Oliver

Demon's Obsession

Controller's Obsession

Christa's Obsession

Secretary's Obsession out March 2025

King's Obsession out May 2025

Little Paws Haven Series

Little Treasure he Hides

Little & Lethal

Enforcers Little Warrior coming April 2025

Divergent Omegaverse Series

Alphas Divergent Omega

Taylin's Temptation due Oct 2024

Booker's Bliss due Jan 2025

Spin off Series in the Divergent Omegaverse Darling Ranch

Ranch-Down coming Feb 2025

The Potters Creek Series

A Christmas Wish (book one)

The App Series

The App: Daddy kink (book one)

The App: Littles (book two)

The App: Puppy play (book three)

The Flamingo Bar Series

Always More (book one)

The Little Side of Me (book two)

3 Is the Magic Number (book three)

La Trattoria Di Amore Series

Puzzle Pieces (book one)

Dominated but not Subdued (book two)

Made to Submit

The Playroom Series

Mine, Body and Soul: Part One

Mine, Body and Soul: Part Two

Mine, Body and Soul: Part Three

Ferron's Journey: Damaged Part One (book four)

Ferron's Journey: Hidden Part Two (book five)

Ferron's Journey: Revelation Part Three (book six)

Mine, Body and Soul Trilogy

Ferron's Journey Trilogy

Spinoff Love's Heart Print

Dark River Stone Collective Series

The Light Beneath the Dark (Book One)

When Darkness Turns to Light (Book Two)

Running From Darkness (Book Three)

The Billionaire Playground Series

Property of a Billionaire (Book one)

Reluctant Billionaire (Book two)

Billionaire's Muse (Book three)

Heart Stones Series

Blood King

The Manx Cat Guardians Series

Where it all Began: Origins (Book 1)
Seeing Beyond the Scars (Book 2)
Destiny Collides Past and Present (Book 3)
Searching for a Soul to Love (Book 4)
The 12 Disasters of Christmas (Book 5)
Laws of Attraction (Book 6)
The Teacher's Boy (Book 7)
Boxset

Weird & Wacky Shifters

All he wants is a Fingerling

Alphas Fingerling Surprize

A Boy Called Blu

The Rhubarb Effect spin off from Weird & Wacky Shifters

Sticky For You

Rhubarb 2 Go

Ravished By the Rhubarb

Embracing The Stalk

Rhubarb Blush

Audio Books

Mine, Body and Soul, Part One: The Playroom Series

Mine, Body and Soul, Part Two: The Playroom Series

Mine, Body and Soul, Part Three: The Playroom Series

Daddy Kink: The App (book one)

Always More: The Flamingo Bar (book one)

When Fake Changed Everything

Ferron's Journey: Damaged Part One

Ferron's Journey: Hidden Part Two

Ferron's Journey: Revelation Part Three

Romance books in a mixed series of M/F and M/M by the Author under a different pen name Jayne Paton

Smith's Corner

Delilah & Dallas (book one)

Layla & Levi (Book two)

Ash & Alora (Book three)

Fox & Faith (book four)

Storm & Stone (book five)

Hunter & Holden (book six)

Crime and Thrillers by the Author under a different pen name J Paton

Headspace

Chozen: Dark MM Crime Drama (Headspace Book 1)

Chozen: Dark MM Crime Drama (Headspace Book 2)

www.ingramcontent.com/pod-product-compliance
Lightning Source LLC
Chambersburg PA
CBHW020735250626
47155CB00003B/771